Mary Elizabeth Herbert

A Search After Sunshine

Algeria in 1871

Mary Elizabeth Herbert

A Search After Sunshine
Algeria in 1871

ISBN/EAN: 9783337288044

Printed in Europe, USA, Canada, Australia, Japan

Cover: Foto ©Andreas Hilbeck / pixelio.de

More available books at **www.hansebooks.com**

ALGERIA IN 1871

OLD ALGIERS

A SEARCH AFTER SUNSHINE

OR

ALGERIA IN 1871

BY

LADY HERBERT

TUNIS LAMP IN GREEN POTTERY

LONDON

RICHARD BENTLEY & SON, NEW BURLINGTON STREET

𝔓𝔲𝔟𝔩𝔦𝔰𝔥𝔢𝔯𝔰 𝔦𝔫 𝔒𝔯𝔡𝔦𝔫𝔞𝔯𝔶 𝔱𝔬 𝔥𝔢𝔯 𝔐𝔞𝔧𝔢𝔰𝔱𝔶

1872

TO MY ELDEST DAUGHTER

LADY MARY HERBERT

—

THIS ACCOUNT OF THE

TRAVELS AND ADVENTURES IN WHICH SHE SHARED

IS

𝔄𝔣𝔣𝔢𝔠𝔱𝔦𝔬𝔫𝔞𝔱𝔢𝔩𝔶 𝔇𝔢𝔡𝔦𝔠𝔞𝔱𝔢𝔡

CONTENTS.

LIST OF ILLUSTRATIONS

(*Engraved by* G. PEARSON).

ALGERIA IN 1871.

CHAPTER I.

ORAN AND TLEMCEN.

UCH has been written and said about this country; but like all colonies, its position is hourly changing, so that its history, written ten or twelve or even five or six years ago, is no longer a true picture of the existing state of things. Moreover, judging by myself, a vague idea exists in England of its inhabitants and configuration. I knew that the French territory in North Africa consisted of three provinces: Oran, Algiers, and Constantine. But I did not know till I went there, that nature had divided the country into certain distinct zones, parallel to the sea, and each having its peculiar character.

The first is the *Sahel* or Sea Shore—the centre of commerce, and the site of most of the principal towns.

B

The second is the *Tell*, or the vast fertile plains
which stretch from the Sahel to the mountainous
ranges of the Atlas.

The third, called by the French, the *Hauts Plateaux*,
consists entirely of mountains and ravines, cultivated
here and there, but mainly used for pasture.

The fourth is the *Sahara* or Desert, wide tracts of
sandy soil, with oases of palms and little mud villages,
the inhabitants of which depend for their very existence on the carefully managed irrigation of their palm
groves.

Again, I had imagined that the native inhabitants
were all Arabs, although, of course, of different tribes.
But I found that the races inhabiting these different
zones were as distinct as the districts themselves.

It is true that after the overthrow of the Romans
and the cruel invasion of the Vandals, the Arabs in
their turn took possession of the sea-coast, and that
80,000 men, despatched by the Caliph Omar in A.D.
645, overran the country, and compelled the inhabitants
to accept the religion of the Prophet.

But they never succeeded in conquering the Kabyles,
or Berbers (who are of Canaanitish origin with a fusion
of Vandal blood) ; and who, retiring into the mountains,
contrived to maintain their independence, and never
submitted to the Arab yoke, though they conformed to
the religion of the conquerors. Again, when in the

sixteenth century Algeria became a province of the Porte, the Kabyles successfully resisted the imposition of Turkish taxes.

Their language is entirely distinct from the Arabic, and they are an industrious race, living in settled homes and not in tents, cultivating the soil with the utmost care, and passionately attached to their native mountains. Besides these two aboriginal races, there are the Moors, or Arabs, dwelling in cities; the Koulourlis, who are the offspring of Turkish fathers and Moorish mothers; the Negros from the interior of Africa; and the Jews, who form a very large proportion of the population of Algiers itself. But of all these different people I shall speak by-and-bye.

Being anxious to judge for myself as to this country and especially to test the efficacy of certain warm springs, which had been strongly recommended to me by a Paris doctor for rheumatism, I started last January with my eldest daughter by the P. and O. steamer 'Bangalore' for Gibraltar, the journey through France being rendered well nigh impossible owing to the war.

I am not going to describe the passage, which was as disagreeable as a head wind and a pitching boat could make it. The vessel was crowded with Indian passengers, and, strangely enough for an outward-bound ship, with a multitude of babies, who screamed literally

day and night.   I was too ill to leave my berth for the
first four days; and on the sixth we arrived at
Gibraltar, and landed in company with an old gentleman who had been set upon by the blacks at Jamaica
at the time of Governor Eyre's mutiny, his head
cut open and he left for dead, while the friend in
whose house he was staying was murdered with all
his family.

On making our way up the narrow semi-English
street which leads to the Club-House Hotel, our
courier met us with dismay, to tell us that not a room
was to be had either there or at any other hotel in the
place, but that we must go into the coffee-room till he
could hunt for a lodging. We were sitting disconsolately enough in the hall, when suddenly the kind-
hearted Governor appeared (General Sir Fenwick
Williams, of Kars) and insisted upon our coming and
taking up our abode in his house, or the 'Convent,'
as the Government House is called, having been
originally a Franciscan monastery. We found afterwards that he had actually given up his own bed-room
and dressing-room for our use, as his hospitable house
was already full; but this was only a sample of the
kindness shown to us during the whole time we waited
at Gibraltar for means to continue our journey. At
last we found that a little French steamer, the 'Spahis,'
started every fortnight for Oran; and through the

kindness of the very agreeable French Consul, the
Vicomte de Fontaine, berths were secured in her for
February 2. But my usual bad luck as to the sea
awaited me. When the morning came, it blew a gale
with torrents of rain; and though we braved it and
went on board, we soon found that there was no chance
of the little vessel getting out of the harbour that day.
Sir Fenwick had anticipated this, and sent his gig to
fetch us ashore again, which we were only too thankful
to do, so as to escape the pitching and tossing of the
next twelve hours. By the following morning, however, the sea was calmer, and at six o'clock we steamed
out of the harbour, and arrived in thirty-six hours at
Nemours, the first town we came to on the African
coast. We had both been ill, as usual; and the food
was so bad, that had it not been for the hamper
which Sir Fenwick Williams had so considerately sent
on board for us, and the contents of which lasted us
during several weeks of our African wanderings, we
should have been in still more dismal plight. Our one
consolation was a beautiful little Italian greyhound,
named 'Coquet,' who laid on our berths and was as
playful as a kitten.

Nemours was once the old Arab port of 'Djemma-
Razaouat' (or the 'Mosque of Pirates'), now a
commonplace little French town used as a depôt for
the Commissariat, and re-christened (according to a

French habit in Algeria, which cannot be too much deprecated) after the Duc de Nemours, when the place was evacuated by the defeated troops of Abd-el-Kader. Here this truly great Arab chieftain, dressed in the usual white haïk and double burnous of his tribe, with the camel's hair cord wound round his head, finally surrendered to the Duc d'Aumale; and getting off his favourite black mare, who, like himself, had been wounded in the fight, put her bridle in the Duke's hand, saying gravely, ' This is the last horse I shall ever ride. Take her; and may she bring you good luck!' The thought of this parting and of the fine old chief, whom we had seen at Damascus acting as the champion of the persecuted Christians, redeemed the dulness of the little town itself, which is brand new and has no Moorish or Arabic remains at all, save the ruins of an old fort and castle on the cliffs, which are of quartz and full of crystals glistening like icicles and snow in the hot African sun. We walked up the little street with its inevitable ' Place ' and ' Cafés ' and ' Billiards,' and came to a large building from whence issued a quantity of little native children. This was the convent school of *Les Dames Trinitaires*, a religious order who have undertaken almost all the schools in this province, in which they have upwards of 250 sisters at work. They wear a black-and-white habit with a cross on the breast, like the men of the same order,

ORAN.

and their object is the same, i.e., the redemption of
slaves and captives, and teaching the Arab and Moorish
children.

The mother superior, seeing we were strangers,
kindly invited us in, and offered us coffee. They had
a *salle d'asile* of about 120 little children, and an *école
communale* of fifty great girls—all nice-looking and
orderly, but many of them suffering from diseases of
the eyes. Strolling down again by the sea-shore and
revelling in the hot sun, we came upon a picturesque
group of Arabs just arrived from the interior, with two
or three 'Spahis,' their scarlet cloaks thrown over
their white clothes, all men above six feet high, and
walking with that magnificent air and gait which makes
them appear like true lords of the soil, and shames the
shuffling little Frenchman, or, in fact, any other European who may attempt to walk along side of them.

The unlading of our cargo being completed, we
went on board again, and this time had no reason to
complain of the weather. The sea was like glass,
and the beautiful coast, with its rocky capes and pro-
montories, and its glistening sandy bays, with here and
there a picturesque old Spanish fortress or ruined
mosque crowning the heights above, made us long
to land twenty times ere we reached Oran. It was
midnight before we cast anchor in that busy little
port. The 'Commandant de Place' had sent his boat

to take us ashore and pass our luggage through the
Custom House—thanks again to the kind thoughtful-
ness of the Vicomte de Fontaines, who had written
to him to have everything ready for us. We drove
to the Hôtel de la Paix by a beautiful moonlight, and
with difficulty got a couple of rooms *au troisième.*

Oran was in itself a great disappointment. We
had been reading gorgeous descriptions of its forts
and palaces, especially of the Château-Neuf, the old
residence of the Beys of Oran, which was supposed to
equal the far-famed Palace of Constantine. But the
hand of the French spoiler had been busy everywhere,
and except a couple of old towers, with here and there
an ancient wall or an escutcheon bearing the arms of
Spain, there are no antiquities left—nothing but wide,
commonplace streets and dismal rows of barracks,
looking as if they had been built by the yard, and
one or two new fortresses commanding all the principal
points of the city. It is, in fact, nothing now but a
garrison town, with tall houses built in the usual
French style, and, as we felt, dangerously high when
we remembered the earthquake of 1790.

The morning after our arrival being Sunday, I went
to the Cathedral of St. Louis. This building formed
part of an ancient monastery of the monks of St.
Bernard, who were brought there by Cardinal Ximenes
after he had transformed the mosque into a Christian

church, and dedicated it to 'our Lady of Victories.'
From 1708 to 1732 it was used as a synagogue, and
then fell into ruins, till restored by the French in 1839.
It is in the shape of a long parallelogram, divided
into three aisles, with a deep chancel, on the walls of
which is a fresco-painting by a M. Saint Pierre,
representing the disembarkation of St. Louis at Tunis,
St. Jerome and St. Augustine being likewise depicted
on each side. Above the arch leading to the choir
are the arms of Cardinal Ximenes; and behind the
high altar is a little chapel ornamented in the Louis
XV. style; which is all that remains of the ancient
Bernardine church. An organ, with vertical or fan-
like pipes, after the Spanish fashion, built at Valencia,
is placed over the entrance-door. All this I saw at
my leisure; but my first impression of the cathedral
was that of the most densely-packed masses of children
I ever beheld. I was not surprised afterwards, when
I visited the *Dames Trinitaires* in their large and
airy convent schools, near the cathedral, to find that
they had 1,500 children under instruction, the greater
portion of whom were crowded into the cathedral for
the High Mass. On my return to the hotel, I found
the English Consul, who is a Genoese, and who most
civilly undertook to arrange everything for our journey
to Tlemcen. The 'Commandant de Place' next appeared with the offer of his open carriage to see the

town, which we gratefully accepted, and all the more
gladly as there were no little carriages to be had in
the place. He took us all round the forts till we came
to the suburb of Kerguenta, which is called the
'Negro Village,' though in reality the refuge of all
the native tribes whom French civilisation has driven
out of the city. Here we got out and walked through
its streets, which are composed of mud walls, without
roofs, and utterly miserable. The Arab inhabitants
were squatted at their doors, or on ledges round the
enclosures, cross-legged, smoking their long pipes, and
enveloped from head to foot in their white 'haïks.'
They looked sullen, poor, and wretched. Sundry
lanky, half-starved dogs and raw-boned donkeys completed the melancholy picture. It was a relief to
drive back to the Boulevard Oudinot, which is prettily
planted with trees at the foot of the old Kasba ; and
then to walk in the 'Promenade de Létang,' a shady
and beautiful walk round the fortifications of the
Château-Neuf, bright with flowers and tropical shrubs,
and commanding a fine view over the surrounding
country.

Returning to the Rue Philippe, we came upon a
beautiful little minaret, octagon in shape, and exquisitely
carved, forming an angle in an old Moorish wall. On
passing through the open door, we found ourselves in a
marble court, with a fountain in the middle for Mussul-

man ablutions, and an arcade round, with rows of double columns; the walls bright with 'azulejos' (coloured tiles highly varnished), and the arches carved in delicate lace-like patterns. This court led into the mosque, which was in the same style, the recess or 'mihrab,' where the pulpit stands, being also richly decorated. Two or three Arabs were praying in one corner with the usual prostrations, and, as our guide informed us, muttering curses on us for our intrusion into their sanctuary. There is one other important mosque left in Oran, that of the saint, Sidi El Hâouri, about whom wonderful miracles are related; one alone will suffice as a specimen of the legends which form part of the teaching of these people, very much as the lives of the saints do in Italy and Spain.

It was during the time of the war between the Moors and Spain, when one day a devout and holy woman came to Sidi El Hâouri to complain that her son had been taken prisoner and carried off to Andalusia as a slave. El Hâouri told her to pray to God with faith, and in the meantime to bring him a dish of broth with meat in it, which the poor mother joyfully did. Now El Hâouri had a favourite greyhound, who was at that moment suckling her young ones. He took the dog on his knees, spoke to her, and gave her the food the woman had brought. Instantly the dog started off, ran to the fort, and got on board a vessel bound for the Spanish coast. No sooner had she landed than she met the young man in question, who was returning from market with some meat which he had been buying for his master. The dog made a great bound, tore the meat out of his hand, and rushed to the shore, the Arab youth following and pursuing her on board a vessel which was just getting under weigh for Oran. The lad recognised the dog as one belonging to the saint, and quickly concealing himself among the cargo, landed safely on his native shores. The dog ran home to her master and her little ones, and the poor mother, with tears of joy, recounted how, by the prayers of the saint and the intelligence of the dog, her son had been safely restored to her.

Allowing for a little Eastern exaggeration, and with the firmest belief in the more than instinct of dogs, we did not think this little story so very improbable.

There is one beautiful walk at Oran to the fort of 'Santa Cruz,' perched on the highest point of the mountains behind the town, and commanding a view over the whole country and the seaboard; so that on clear days you can distinguish the coast of Carthagena. It is a terribly steep climb up to the top, but the panorama repays you for the trouble. A few feet below is a pretty little chapel built in 1849, as a thanksgiving for the cessation of the cholera, and which has been ever since a favourite place of pilgrimage.

The following morning we resolved to make a pic-
nic expedition to Mers-el-Kebir, a picturesque old
brown fortress built by the Moors during their occupation of Spain, and used by them as a port for the greater
part of their commercial transactions with Europe.
Afterwards it became a very nest of pirates, but since
the French occupation of the country it has been
turned into a military prison. Passing through a
tunnel, the roof of which was covered with fossil
bivalves, we drove along a road lately made by the
French engineers round the edge of the bay, till we
came to the thermal springs of Jane, daughter of
Queen Isabella of Castile, which are still used by the
Arabs (especially in cutaneous diseases), and very
generally resorted to in summer by the inhabitants of
Oran. Following a little path, only wide enough for
one person at a time, we came to a grotto in the heart
of the quartz rock, from which the spring rushed out
into a basin at the rate of 250 quarts a minute. The
water is clear and limpid, but rather salt. There is
a tidy little bathing establishment below, divided into
two parts, one containing eight or ten separate bathing
places, the other fitted up for douches, &c. For the
benefit of medical men, I give Dr. Bertherand's analysis
of these waters, which, he says, are very useful in all
rheumatic affections.

Water .	.	.	.	.	.	.	1000 grs.
Chloride of Soda .	.	.	.	.	.	.	5,956
—— of Magnesia	.	.	.	.	.	.	4,317
Sulphate of Magnesia .	.	.	.	.	.	.	420
Carbonate of Lime	.	.	.	.	.	.	1,078
Silex .	.	.	.	.	.	.	809
							12,580

From the thermal springs we drove on to St.
André, a pretty little fishing village, where the whole
population seemed to be engaged in drawing in a huge
netful of sardines, a shoal of these fish having appeared at the mouth of the bay. It was a most
exciting moment; men, women, and children, screaming and hauling at the ropes, half in and half out of the
water. The men, dressed in brilliant yellow kilts and
scarlet caps, the former of so lovely a shade that M——
longed to buy them on the spot. Ten minutes' drive
from St. André brought us to the old fortress, built on
a spit of land running out into the sea like a natural
jetty. At the entrance is an old Moorish fountain,
surmounted with the arms of Ferdinand of Arragon,
while over the venerable gateway, and let into the
walls of the various towers, are a number of old Latin
and Spanish inscriptions, recording the names of the
different kings or governors who had occupied this
fortress in the sixteenth and seventeenth centuries.
In fact, Mers-el-Kebir, which was the *Portus Divinus*
of the Romans, has passed through as many hands as

there have been conquerors of North Africa, and its architecture is a medley of them all—part Roman, part Moorish, part Spanish, part Turk, and now almost wholly French! A civil engineer officer showed us over the whole building, including the military prison, which I thought dreary in the extreme. The sentence of the prisoners varied from two to five years, and their only recreation seemed to be a short walk round a bastion at one angle of the fortress looking on the sea. But I could not awaken any sympathy for their fate in the mind of my guide, whose motto was, 'La discipline avant tout.' The old man was very proud of his fortress, and exclaimed, when pointing to the vast extent of seaboard which the eye travelled over from the telegraph tower at the extreme end of the enclosure; 'Ah! ces gredins de Prussiens! Qu'ils montrent le nez seulement sur l'horizon!' pointing expressively to the big guns which lay, as it were, sleeping in their embrasures. We found that the belief that the Prussians would try to take possession of Algeria was universal among French military men at that time, and not wishing to disturb the complacency of our guide, or spoil his faith in his big guns, we remained silent, and walked gravely back towards the entrance-gate, where we parted, the veteran indignantly declining the five-franc piece I tendered, with the words: 'Pardon, madame, on ne paie pas cet honneur;' and, making us a military salute, withdrew.

The next day we drove a little way outside the town to pay our respects to the bishop, Monseigneur Callot, to whom I had a letter of introduction, picking up on our way a sister who was going to him on business. His little country house was simple in the extreme, and his chapel scarcely large enough for his modest household; but he had a beautiful garden at the back, into which he took us, to show us a finely-carved statue of 'Notre Dame de Fourvières,' which he had brought with him from Lyons, his native place. He gave us a terrible account of the Arab famine three years ago, which had decimated the inhabitants of Oran, and of which we heard still more fearful reports in Algiers. Fever, as usual, had followed in its wake. The bishop pitched a number of tents on the open space near Mers-el-Kebir, and there, with four or five of his priests, fed and watched over the dying and the dead, and that in thousands. He said it was horrible to see the children fighting for the oats which had dropped out of the bottom of the sack in which his horse had been fed. But in spite of all their efforts, the mortality was fearful. One of his priests was among the victims of this heroic charity. The little orphans were placed by him under the care of the sisters at Misserghin, which is the first stage from Oran to Tlemcen, and whose ' Home' he begged me to go and see. The gathering of the 'helfeh' grass, much used in paper and other manufactures, as well as for matting, and which is a principal export from the port of Oran, was, he told us, one of the main sources of revenue to the orphanage. On our return, we went into the only good curiosity shop in Oran, and got a large mat of this very 'helfeh' grass, some pretty cheap green Moorish pots, and an old shawl of that peculiar kind worn by the Jewish women, and which is of an exquisite shade of crimson.

That night we started by diligence for Tlemcen, not without some reluctance; but we had no choice. Even if a private carriage could have been obtained at Oran, there were no horses; and sundry uncomfortable rumours of hostile Arabs made us feel that it would not be well to travel alone. And in truth, with the exception of the two or three post-houses or stations where the horses are changed, it is impossible to conceive anything more lonely and deserted than this road. For miles and miles, it runs through an undulating but gently ascending plain of dwarf palm trees (the Chamærops or fan palm), wild squill and genista. There is no cultivation whatever, save a little patch here and there near the wayside caravanserai, which are enclosed by a high wall for defence from both man and beast. Not a living thing was to be seen, nor a

human habitation, save the post-houses above named.
The night was lovely, a brilliant moon lit up the
dreary plain, through which we drove for seventeen or
eighteen hours, till the sameness and stillness filled one
with a nameless fear. I once saw a picture of the
world before the creation of man—a vast sea of
verdure, with here and there a wild beast feeding.
But here, there was not even a wild beast! though
occasionally a jackal's unearthly cry broke the awful
stillness of the night: and once, the glare of a pine
torch revealed an Arab tent, with the crouching
figures wrapped in their burnouses, looking ghost-like
amidst the flickering shadows.

About half-way, we passed the great Salt Lake of
Sebkhra which is of an immense extent, and is formed
by a sheet of water which the heat in summer
evaporates, leaving a bed of crystallised deposits,
glittering, as we saw it, in the moonlight. Towards
morning we came to Ain Tekbalet, close to which are
the quarries of Oriental alabaster, from whence were
obtained those beautiful pillars which form the glory of
the Basilica of S. Paolo fuore-le-mure at Rome. It is
a description of onyx, of a most delicate and transparent colour, varying in shade from deep orange to
pale yellow, white, and even pink. The French use it
for every description of table ornament; and in sheets,
for fire-screens, &c.

From Ain Tekbalet, the road rises and winds through a mountainous ravine, till a sudden turn reveals the most beautiful panorama possible, which was all the more unexpected from the monotony of the previous route. A high chain of mountains, still in deep purple shadow, bounded the horizon ; while through the plain at our feet, studded with olive and orange groves, the bright stream of the Isser flowed rapidly ; and the town of Tlemcen, the ancient capital of the Marreb and the key of the west, with its picturesque mosque, crenelated walls, high Moorish towers, circular tombs or 'koubbas,' and horse-shoe arched gateways sparkled like a gem in the rising sun. Our sleepless night, cramped position, and weary aching limbs were all forgotten as this enchanting view burst upon us, and we had hardly patience with the tired horses, who were dragging us slowly and painfully across the picturesque bridge and up the steep ascent leading to the Oran Gate of the grand old city. We found two queer little rooms, only accessible by an outside staircase, prepared for us in the Hôtel de France, whose landlord had dispossessed an unhappy French officer for our benefit ; for in a very few moments a civil orderly knocked at my door humbly to beg for 'le sabre et les bottes de monsieur le capitaine,' of which, in his hurried flitting, I had unconsciously become the temporary possessor.

We had been provided with sundry letters of introduction from the consul at Oran to the notabilities of
Tlemcen, and having shaken off the dust of the
diligence, and engaged the only little carriage to be
found in the city (which was of a most original description), we drove out of the gates again to the
house of a M. Gués, who had a villa in one of the
orange groves which surround the town, very much
like those at Sidon in Syria. M. Gués was laid up
with the gout, and unable, to our great regret, to do
the honours of his adopted country ; but he most
good naturedly lent us his servant to be our cicerone
and interpreter, and hobbled himself into the garden to
give us a magnificent bouquet of roses and Neapolitan
violets, only regretting that we had come too early in
the season for choicer flowers. Our Arab guide
sprang quickly on the box, and directed our driver to
take us first to the village of El Eubbad, or Sidi-Bou-
Medin, the picturesque white minaret of which had
already attracted our attention. The road led us
through the Arab cemetery, and by a succession of
olive groves very like Mentone, till we came to the
foot of the village. Here we left the carriage and
climbed up the steep, deserted-looking street of mud
houses without roofs, until we came to a wooden door
covered with coloured arabesques, which led into a
square portico paved with glazed tiles and leading to

the mosque on the right, and the Koubba or tomb of
the saint Sidi-Bou-Medin to the left. Descending a few
steep steps we came into an outer court, or what
would be called a *patio* in Spain, surrounded with
arcades resting on columns of onyx and Oriental
alabaster. In the centre was a beautiful Moorish
fountain, and on a matted stone slab round the wall
were squatted a multitude of young girls, all remark-
ably beautiful, with bright clear skins, dark eyes, and
pencilled eyebrows. Fantastic lanterns hung from the
centre of the arches, and a quantity of cages filled
with singing-birds were suspended from hooks in the
wall, which was likewise decorated with Arabic inscriptions, views of Mecca, and illuminated drawings of
Mahomet's slippers. From this outer court we passed
into an inner chamber containing the tomb of the
saint, which is in sculptured wood covered with the
richest gold and silver stuffs, above which are
hung banners with Arabic inscriptions, ostrich eggs
gaily coloured, and what we should call Paschal
candles. The ceiling and doors were richly carved
and painted in Arabesque and Cufic characters. The
light was only admitted by narrow carved stone slits
of windows, which were filled with stained glass. A
variety of coloured lanterns, mirrors, and bright
pictures were hung round the walls very much like
ex-votos in Catholic places of pilgrimage. Out of

deference to the feelings of our guide we took off our shoes on entering; but he did not seem satisfied even then, and went on making a variety of salaams with his forehead to the ground on the rich carpet which covered the floor, and occasionally drinking some water from a well to the left, the marble mouth of which was worn by the chain which, six centuries ago, had been placed by pious pilgrims to draw up the water from this sacred spring. Close to this spot is another coffin containing the remains of the chosen disciple and friend of the saint; and to the right of the staircase are interred several other privileged persons who, either from their high birth or eminent piety, have been permitted to mingle their ashes with those of Bou-Medin. It is impossible not to respect the evident faith of these poor people in their traditions, however much one may grieve to see piety so misplaced. Re-ascending the steep steps we crossed the road to the mosque, for the excessive beauty and richness of which we were quite unprepared. A staircase of eleven marble steps under a richly decorated cupola led us to the entrance doors, which are of massive cedar wood, inlaid with lozenge-shaped *plaques* of bronze, on which every kind of device is wrought. The handles, hinges, and locks, are of equally beautiful workmanship, and reveal their Spanish origin, these doors having been the price of a Spaniard's liberty in

the sixteenth century. To the right of this doorway
is the minaret, covered externally with glazed tiles, up
which we scrambled, and were repaid by a glorious
view over the surrounding country. Retracing our
steps, we came into a large square court, surrounded
by arcades supported on marble pillars with the
invariable fountain in the centre for ablutions; and
then entered the mosque itself, which appeared to be
absolutely a bit of the Alhambra. There were the
same lace-like edges to the arches, the same inter-
section of columns, the same exquisitely carved dome
and walls covered with an infinite variety of patterns.
The 'mihrab' or Holy of Holies, with its onyx
columns, was, of course, the *chef-d'œuvre* of the
whole; and the 'minbar' or pulpit was beautifully
carved in cedar-wood. And this description will
serve for all the other mosques in Tlemcen; although
none are so richly and beautifully decorated throughout. We talked to the Dervish who had been our
guide and was also the village schoolmaster. He took
us to see the 'medresa' or college, which is connected
with the mosque by a cloister, into which all the cells
of the students open. But it is now empty and
neglected, with only a few sculptures on the walls to
tell of its past glories. Boys only, receive instruction
in this village. 'Girls do not need it; they have no
souls; they die like the dog!' was the commentary of

our guide to my inquiry as to the education given to the women. They certainly were beautiful enough to deserve a better fate.

Returning towards the town, we passed again through the Arab burial-ground, full of beautiful and picturesque 'koubbas' or circular tombs, their little domes shaded by venerable olive trees often of a great size; and went on to the mosque of *Sidi El-Haloui.* He may be called the patron saint of Tlemcen and his story is as follows. He was born at Seville, where he became a Kadi; when, all of a sudden, leaving his home, his honours, and his fortune, he started as a pilgrim for Africa and arrived at Tlemcen. There he opened a stall of bon-bons and sweet things (called *Halaouat*), which he gave to the children, who bestowed upon him the nick-name of ' Haloui ;' and when he had sufficiently attracted their attention by his sweetmeats and his buffoonery, he suddenly changed his tone and began to preach to them and to the quickly gathering crowd, and that with such eloquence that the whole town was converted. Tidings of his miracles coming to the ear of the Sultan, he was chosen as tutor to his sons. But this appointment giving umbrage to the grand vizier, he was accused as a sorcerer, tried, condemned, and beheaded outside the gates. The evening of this terrible execution, which had roused the public indignation to the utmost extent, the ' bououab,' or guardian of the gates, was crying as usual to the laggards outside to come in before the doors were closed, when a sepulchral voice was heard exclaiming : 'Close thy gates, Bououab! There is no one with- out, save El-Haloui, the oppressed!' For seven days this same voice was heard, repeating the self-same words. The people openly murmured. The Sultan came himself to the gates, and when he returned to his palace exclaimed : '*I wished to hear, I have heard.*' The next morning, the vizier was put to death on the very spot where El-Haloui had been beheaded, by being buried alive in a block of mortar : and to appease the saint, a beautiful mosque was built over his tomb which remains to this day. It contains some fine Oriental alabaster columns, but its minaret, covered with coloured tiles, is its chief attraction. A stork had built her nest on the top and was sitting on her eggs, her mate gravely perched beside her. Close by, is a purely negro village, out of which swarmed a multitude of little naked woolly-headed creatures to stare at the strangers. Another mosque with a graceful minaret is built just beyond El-Haloui's tomb, but it appeared to be deserted.

Leaving our carriage at the fine horse-shoe arched gates, we now determined to explore the town and walk through its bazaars. But except one or two of those same red shawls such as we had seen at

Oran, and an enormous Palmetto hat, there was
nothing at first sight very tempting or attractive;
while the prices asked were exorbitant. Coming into
a little square or 'place' where a quantity of the
cochineal-dyed wool for these native shawls was
hanging in the sun, we saw a troop of Arab children
going through a low door-way, whom we followed and,
to our surprise, came into a beautiful little mosque
intersected by horse-shoe arches and onyx columns,
which had been converted into an Arabic and French
College. The 'mihrab' remains, the dome and sides
of which are covered with the most beautiful and
exquisite carvings; so that it was impossible not to
regret its conversion into an ordinary day-school.

The principal mosque of the city, however, is that
of Djama Kebir, the outer court of which is paved
with alabaster, the fountain in the centre being of the
same material. The interior, which is very large, has
been ruthlessly whitewashed, and nothing remains of
its ancient colours or magnificence, save the 'mihrab'
which is still decorated in Saracenic fashion. The
minaret is covered with tiles of that beautiful blueish
green, the art of making which seems now to be
extinct. The king who built it was asked to add an
inscription at the base of the tower recording the fact.
But he replied: 'No, *God* knows it!' a sentiment
worthy of the imitation of some Christians.

About three kilomètres from the town, there is a most curious ruin called Mansoura, which looks like the ghost of a deserted city. About a hundred acres of ground have been enclosed by crenelated ramparts of that reddish brown 'tufa' so familiar to travellers in the Campagna of Rome, with a multitude of towers at regular distances, and a minaret forty-five feet high to the west of the battlements, constructed of those narrow tiled bricks, so common in early Roman architecture, and covered with varnished tiles ; the richly laced archway with its onyx columns still bearing the name of the sultan who erected it. This curious town called El-Mansoura or the Victorious was built by Abou Yakoub in the thirteenth century, when he besieged Tlemcen. The siege lasted eight years ; and this sultan having vowed to reduce the town to submission, and wishing to be comfortable in the meanwhile, caused this great city to be constructed, for himself and his army, with baths, mosques, and all the appliances of Eastern civilisation. But when Tlemcen had yielded and opened her gates to the conqueror, Mansoura was abandoned. Abou Yakoub, however, did not witness this triumph of his arms, having been assassinated by a slave before the surrender of the town.

The guide-books speak of a multitude of alabaster columns and interesting inscriptions to be found in

the ruined city; but all these have now, most unfortunately, been transported to Algiers, and only a
few of the mural tablets to the museum at Tlemcen.
But enough remains to give this ghost-like old city
a *cachet* of its own, and we wandered in and out of
its silent fortifications, musing on the extraordinary
perseverance and determination of the old chieftain
who had resorted to so marvellous an expenditure in
order to accomplish his purpose.   On our return to
Tlemcen, we hunted out an old photographer named
Pedra, living in a villanous side street, but who was
the only person of whom we could obtain any views
of the town.   He was a great character : and having
established us on the only two chairs he possessed,
set us down in the centre of his little court-yard,
threw into our laps a huge roll of photographs without mounts, names, or price, and asked us to take our
choice, while he manipulated a shy private of the
'Chasseurs d'Afrique' who had come to be immor-
talised for his *chère amie.*   We chose about twenty,
for which he charged an absurdly small sum ; all the
while going on with running comments on his sitter
in the most amusing fashion, till the poor man fairly
bolted, muttering that he would return another day.

Tired and wearied with sight seeing, I left M—— at
the hotel, and strolled down to the Catholic church,
which is just outside the town, and is a very beautiful

building in the Norman style. I was struck there, as I was throughout my travels in Algeria, with the care with which the French have built churches and established schools (under the direction of the different Orders of sisters or brothers of charity), wherever they have a military station or even a small number of colonists. Dr. Bennett, in his 'Winter on the Shores of the Mediterranean' speaks of this trait in the French character with positive enthusiasm. He writes :—

'The settlement of the French in Algeria, although certainly undertaken and continued for political and military purposes, has also, in reality, a decided missionary character. It is the first grand inroad made on the headquarters of Mahometan infidelity since the time of the Crusaders. The gain is the gain of Christianity and of civilisation, and all the Christian nations of Europe ought to feel that they owe a debt of gratitude to France for what she has accomplished in Algeria, and be willing to help her in her great enterprise.'

From the church, where we had a beautiful Benediction at a lovely alabaster altar, I walked to see the sisters of charity or 'les dames Trinitaires,' but I found them in some trouble. It was a moment of revolution, and the battle of 'Secular Education *versus* Religious' was being fought as vigorously in North Africa as it is now in England. The success of the ultra Liberal party in France had emboldened the 'Rouges' in Algeria, and they had closed the fine school-rooms of the 'Commune,' and prohibited the sisters from attending them. The parents, however, were of a different opinion from the municipality, and sent their children to the sisters in preference to the new secular Teachers. So the poor little things were all huddled into an unwholesome small house and court, instead of being in the fine class rooms which had been built for them by the previous government. The same thing happened with the boys' schools kept by the Christian Brothers, and to the great wrath of the authorities, the children all crowded into the 'Brothers'' private houses, where they were ejected several times, but in vain. The boys *would* follow the Brothers, and by their obstinacy eventually gained the day.

Among our letters of introduction we had brought one for M. de Siegnette, the head of the 'Bureau Arabe,' and the French military interpreter; a most gentlemanlike, intelligent man, who had seen a great deal of service, and gave us every kind of interesting information about the people and country. He volunteered the following morning to ride with us to the cascades of El-Ourit, which are about six miles from the town. The road winds through a beautiful and picturesque valley full of orchards and orange groves, cherry trees in full blossom, oleanders and spring flowers, backed by a magnificent chain of mountains which at the waterfall itself, form themselves into a circular mass of reddish stone, inaccessible save to the goats. The falls reminded me of Terni, the waters rushing over the rocks at intervals, and occasionally quite hidden by the luxuriant vegetation clothing the hill-side, and which, a little later in the year, must be quite beautiful. As it was, the tender green of the spring leaves, seen here and there through the rainbow caused by the sun's rays on the falling water, gave to the whole scene a beautifully misty and fairy-like effect which will ever remain on my memory. We dismounted and stood on the bridge looking up at the falls, and then scrambled into some caverns at the side, full of exquisite ferns ; while the little goat-herds, at a word from M. de Siegnette, brought us great bunches of sweet double violets. He told us that during the cherry season, the whole population of Tlemcen flocked into this valley and often tented out here for several days. We were accompanied by M. de Siegnette's Spahis servant, in his full Arab dress and scarlet cloak, which led to a talk about their corps. M. de Siegnette said that their means of communication with each other were incredible : that they had, like the sepoys in India, a kind of 'underground railway' by which they knew everything that was

passing long before the Europeans. The week before, there had been a revolt of the Spahis at Souk
Harras, on the borders of Tunis, and the officers at
Tlemcen had only just heard of it; though they discovered that the whole plot had been discussed by
their Spahis guards, who knew of the attempt and its
failure before any rumour of either had reached the
authorities. This gives the French officers a great
feeling of insecurity, as no real fidelity can be expected
of their men; and at any moment, when the chances
of success are in their favour, they may rise against
them. We had not time, to our great regret, to go on
to the palm forest or to visit the grottos beyond, of
which we had bought some tempting photographs; so
we contented ourselves with visiting some of the
picturesque horse-shoe arched 'koubbas' on our way
back; and then going over the *Mechouar*, or ancient
palace of the Emirs, of which little remains at present
save the magnificent old walls, gateway, and mosque.
The French have treated the place ruthlessly and
converted the most interesting portions of the palace
into barracks and hospitals. M. de Siegnette next
took us into the museum, where Mr. C. Brosselard has
collected all the antiquities he could rescue from the
vandalism of the French soldiers, though the most
interesting have been transported to the museum at
Algiers. There are, however, one or two beautiful

Oriental alabaster columns from the *Mechouar*, and a
good many Roman inscriptions. From the museum,
we wandered into some of the private houses, with
their open 'patios,' and picturesque Moorish arches
and colonnades. One in particular arrested my attention, from its handsome wide flight of steps and beautifully carved gallery round the court, which was
thickly festooned with vine leaves and passion flowers,
hanging in graceful wreaths over the old arches,
waving in the soft spring air, and throwing flickering
shadows on the marble pavement and old well below.
Before I left, I made one more expedition with M. de
Siegnette into the dirty bazaar; where we were invited
to sit behind the counter, and regaled with pipes and
coffee, while we haggled again for the red Tlemcen
shawls, and finally bought one with a gold border at
not much more than twice its value. A panther's
skin was brought in by an Arab whilst we were
squatted there, but it had been riddled by shot, the
man having himself narrowly escaped with his life.
There were heaps of quaint and curious things, which
I should have liked to buy, but was deterred by the
thought of how on earth I should get them home!
Among the rest were some grotesque shaped lamps of
green pottery, of a kind peculiar to the place, and
only costing a few pence. I have always been sorry

afterwards when I have not carried off such reminis-
cences, as they never can be met with elsewhere.

That night we started again for Oran, taking leave
of Tlemcen with real regret.   M. Gués sent us a
beautiful nosegay of Neapolitan violets and roses,
imploring us to return later in the season ; and, with
many such kind farewell wishes echoed by the little
group which surrounded the inn door, we clambered
again into our uncomfortable diligence, which rumbled
slowly down the steep hill, and soon found ourselves
once more driving along the dreary, monotonous fan
palm plain through the long dark night.

At six o'clock in the morning we reached Misserghin,
where I hoped to have stayed and seen the Arab
schools, for which the Bishop of Oran had given me a
letter of introduction.   But, unfortunately, there was
no carriage of any sort to take me on to Oran if I
abandoned the diligence, which only waited to change
horses ; so that very reluctantly I had to content
myself with an outside view of the church and orphanage, and a glimpse of the sisters as they came out of
their house on their way to the early Mass.   I saw
plenty of the like schools afterwards near Algiers ;
but always regretted not having fulfilled my promise
to the good Bishop, and seen this, the only consoling
result in the province of Oran, of what the Arabs call
in their expressive language the ' year of death.'

TLEMCEN. GATEWAY

CHAPTER II.

MILIANA, TENIET-EL-HAD, AND BLIDAH.

T was yet dark when we bid good-bye to Oran, and started by the six o'clock train by the new railroad, which is eventually to connect Oran with Algiers, but which at present, stops short at Lavrande.

The country was one vast uncultivated plain of dwarf fan palms (the 'bush' of Algeria) until we reached Orleansville, when it became wooded and pretty. This modern town is built on the ruins of an old Roman city, and one which is full of interest to the ecclesiastical archæologist. In 1843, a fine basilica was discovered, dedicated to St. Reparatus, with the date of his death, in the year 436 of the Mauritanian era. The mosaic pavement, (red, black and white) was found entire : and various inscriptions, recording the laying of the first stone of the basilica on November 20th, 325, with the words : 'Mente habeas servum Dei,'

. . . . . evidently referring to the founder, whose name has been erased by time; and the slab of a marble altar, on which is engraved : 'Beatis Apostolis Petro et Paulo;' while the words 'Sancta Ecclesia' and 'Saturninus Sacerdos' are repeated in various places, as if they referred to the bishop, in whose time the basilica was consecrated. Such a number of Christian inscriptions are rare in this country, but the greater portion have been transported to the Museum at Algiers.

Our travelling companion was the Prefect of Oran, who had just been appointed Governor of Algeria, *a rouge* of the first water, who believing me to be a Protestant as well as an Englishwoman, gave free vent to his opinions on religion and education, with which I need not say I had no sympathy whatever. This gentleman had been a clerk to the Mayor of Constantine only a few months before ; and his rapid promotion gave rise to many ill-natured comments. But although his principles were diametrically opposed to my own, I am bound to say that he was singularly courteous and kind to us, and afterwards was the means of our visiting an interesting portion of the province of Constantine in a very agreeable manner.

The road now ran through the fertile and beautiful valley of the Chelif, a rapid river which we followed all the way to Miliana. At Lavrande, (so called because it was the name of a general killed at Sevastopol) we left the train and got into an omnibus, which was to convey us the last remaining twelve kilomètres to our destination.

After leaving Affreville, where there was a crowded Arab market, the road suddenly turned and wound up a magnificent gorge, (so steep that it seemed like going up the side of a house), by the side of a rushing mountain torrent, mountains hemming us in on all sides, and picturesque mills and bridges at intervals spanning the stream, while winding zigzag paths appeared, now on our left and now on our right, as we struggled up the terrible ascent. It was a grander edition of the scenery near Chaude-Fontaine and Liége. Half way up, we stopped at an Arab caravanserai, for the horses to rest and breathe a little; and there saw a multitude of Arabs, all squatted close together in a long low hut, drinking coffee and beating time to the monotonous sound of a tum-tum—a sight which became familiar enough to us at Tunis later in the year, but which then seemed novel and strange. It was ten o'clock at night before we reached the comfortable little Hôtel d'Isly at Miliana, as from the terrible steepness of the ascent, we had been four hours doing the last eight miles! A homely, good-natured Frenchwoman brought us some excellent hot soup in the little coffee-room of her primitive hotel, and ushered us into two beautifully clean bed-rooms, with bright fires of vine branches crackling on the hearth—a luxury which the cold of this high region made very acceptable.

The morning sun shone bright and clear, as I made my way the next day, (Sunday), to the little church at the end of the 'Place,' where I found a military mass going on, and, as usual, a perfect army of sisters and children. The rector is the nephew of Monseigneur de Pavy, the late Archbishop of Algiers, and is not only a first-rate preacher, but a most holy and excellent man. After church, M—— and I took a walk over the town. The position is a glorious one : on a high plateau, overlooking a magnificent plain, bounded by high mountains, and many of them covered with snow. From the ramparts, the ground sloped rapidly down towards the road we had ascended the night before, and was covered with vineyards, and peach, almond, apricot, and cherry trees in full blossom, the whole being carefully cultivated in little terrace gardens, irrigated by mountain streams. In the little 'Place,' a minaret has been converted into a clock tower, from which beautiful creepers hung in graceful wreaths. We wandered through the Arab streets, full of picturesque figures and bright coloured stuffs, till we came to a kind of market-place, where a number of camels were patiently squatted on the ground ; occasionally growling—showing their teeth as is their wont, when any attempt was made to replace their loads. A little further on was a beautiful old mosque and a 'koubba,' the last resting-place of Sidi Mohammed-ben-Yussef, a poor but virtuous saint, who was supposed to work miracles ; but who was still more remarkable for certain sarcastic and epigrammatic verses, which have passed into proverbs among the Arabs. He was very, severe against the Miliana women, who, he said, ' usurped the place of men, and commanded when they should rather obey.' So that we see the 'Woman's Rights' question was mooted in this out-of-the-way region four hundred years ago! The outer court of this mosque was arcaded with a double row of columns and horse-shoe arches decorated with curious open-worked tiles. In the centre was the usual fine old marble fountain. The mosque was lined with coloured tiles, and above the tomb waved silk banners, bright lanterns, and ostrich eggs. The ceiling and pulpit were of cedar wood, brightly coloured ; and the outer doors of bronze, with big nails, like those in the gateway at Toledo. In dark mysterious little chambers, all round the court, squatted the Arabs, who made us take off our shoes before entering the holy place, but were not otherwise hostile. I always felt, however, that they were muttering curses upon us when we entered their sanctuaries and that only fear kept them from cutting our throats. Afterwards we walked outside the town towards the mountain of Zakkar by a picturesque plane-tree avenue, on one side of which was a botanical garden. Every description of plant and shrub seems to grow well in this soil; and I no longer wondered at the Archbishop having chosen this fertile, healthy and beautiful region for his infant colony of Arab Christians; but more of that subject by-and-bye.

In the afternoon, I went back to church and, then to see the Sisters of the 'Doctrine Chrétienne,' who have a school here of upwards of three hundred children. The radical municipality had paid a domiciliary visit to their classes that week, and confessed themselves pleased with the progress of the children. But one of them taking up a copy of the New Testament, which one of the girls was learning, exclaimed to the superior : 'You dare to teach this?' The superior calmly replied, 'Sir, I am a religious, and as long as I am here, I shall teach the children religion.' He then began abusing the holy pictures and Crucifixes on the walls, exclaiming, 'Il faut balayer tout cela!' (we must make a clean sweep of all this rubbish). But the rest of the party, ashamed of his violence, and somewhat awed by the quiet, gentle manner of the superior, silenced him and withdrew peaceably, without carrying their threats into execution.

The evening found us again on that beautiful terrace,

overlooking the valley, the setting sun lighting up the Waransenis, with its high peak and long shoulder covered with snow, which is the great landmark of the country ; and with which we were soon to make a nearer acquaintance. I regretted so much not having brought any materials for sketching to Miliana, where such beautiful views are to be met with on all sides. It would be a charming place in which to spend a couple of months in the spring or early summer, with the advantage of being able to live for next to nothing.

Our object now was to get on to Teniet-el-Had, but this was attended with some difficulty. There was only one kind of conveyance, a species of covered cart with very high sides, into which it was almost impossible to stride without having very long legs ; and when inside, it was equally difficult to get out again. Moreover, this primitive conveyance started at midnight, a most inconvenient hour for people who wished to see something of the country. However, finding we had no other alternative, we made up our minds to make the best of it, and groping our way in the dark to the little ' Place,' scrambled with immense difficulty into the cart, which we were told was meant to hold eight persons, though we, four, could hardly sit ; and in this prison we spent fourteen mortal hours, never arriving at Teniet till half-past two o'clock in the afternoon.

Following the same route by which we had arrived to Miliana, we soon descended to Affreville, and there began our troubles.

The first thing to do was to cross the Chelif, which had been so swollen by the late rains that it was a matter of great difficulty. However, after consultation with the ferryman, the two gentlemen of our party went in a boat to lighten the cart, but we had got in with too much difficulty to be willing to turn out without necessity, so stuck to our cranky conveyance; and the driver lashing his horses into a gallop we plunged into the stream, and though the machine was almost knocked to pieces by the big stones at the bottom of the river, we arrived safely at the opposite bank; there was no fear of breaking our springs, for the cart was guiltless of such luxuries. The whole distance to Teniet is done in two stages, although the ascent is tremendous, the roads execrable, and the consequent strain on the horses terrible. The scenery was magnificent, though most desolate. We saw but four little houses the whole way, which were the residences of the *cantonniers*, who are supposed to keep the road in order, though no one would guess it. The ruts were deeper than the axles of the wheels, and how the poor brutes managed to drag us along through such holes and 'sloughs of despond' I cannot imagine. We had a nervous gentleman seated in front with the driver, and

at every lurch he went on invoking all his patron
saints, and promising the Virgin endless candles for
her altar if he only arrived safely at his destination.
Once or twice we were compelled to scramble out of
our cage, and wade through the mud whilst the machine
was being righted, the driver muttering imprecations
on *le génie*, who certainly had not shown much genius
in their care of the road. At about eleven o'clock
we stopped to breakfast at a little wayside caravanserai,
called Anseur-el-Louza, where we got some mountain
red-legged partridges and an omelette. The view from
hence was lovely. The road was bordered by cork
trees, ilex, arbutus, and olives; with the dwarf palm,
wild lavender, rosemary, and other aromatic-smelling
shrubs. A very pretty little white flower, like a single
jonquil, smelling like a narcissus, with a yellow centre,
grew in profusion out of the moss by the roadside. I
was told afterwards that it was peculiar to that part of
the country; but although I brought back some of the
bulbs, they would not grow. The river *l'Oned-Rerga*,
a branch of the Chelif, rushes in a picturesque deep
gorge by the side of the road which, from the caravanserai to Teniet, is like a beautiful alpine pass. Soon
we came upon a group of tents occupied by soldiers,
who were striving to fill up the ruts and improve the
road, though not with much success. Arrived at
Teniet, we found a modern French station, with modern

French houses, a tidy little French church, an ' École communale,' and a convent for the Sisters, but nothing Oriental, save a few Arabs and Spahis lounging in the long village street, and some handsome Jewesses squatted outside their doors in their gorgeous dresses, with masses of gold coins on their necks and arms. Our first arrival was decidedly inauspicious. There was but one little place which could be called an inn, and that was full. The landlady was *désolée*! ' But the season had been so bad ! No one had come on account of the war ; and she had let her only bed-rooms *en permanence* to the officers of the garrison.' However, after some discussion with her daughter, she offered us at last their own bed-rooms, which consisted of two little *lean-tos* at the back of the house, with sloping roofs ; forming in fact one side of a poultry-yard, and leading out of the kitchen. Such as they were, however, we accepted them thankfully, and then joined the company at the primitive *table-d'hôte* dinner, which consisted of our timid friend and fellow-traveller, an Arab sheik, and the officers of the little garrison. Introduced to the colonel, I petitioned for the loan of some horses on the following day to take us to the famous cedar forest, which he at once most good-naturedly promised us, as also an escort and guides, which the depth of the snow rendered absolutely necessary. Without in the least disparaging his kindness, it was evidently a pleasant change in the monotonous lives of these gentlemen to find two ladies to lionise in this out-of-the-way spot, and to be able to hear from them the last European news, which the war had made of all-engrossing interest.

After dinner, I strolled down to the little church, which had a pretty altar of cedar wood, and then to see the Sisters of the ' Doctrine Chrétienne ' and their school. They had a dear little Arab child among the rest, who cried when I asked her if she had been baptised. She is so anxious for it that she is learning her catechism with all her might so as to be ready for Easter. 'Je *veux* être Chrétienne, je veux qu'on me donne le nom de Marie!' she said amidst her sobs. The little ones had all beautiful dark eyes and bright complexions, speaking well for the healthiness of Teniet; but the sisters are sadly cramped for room, and their house is cold and damp. The superior has a brother in the Foreign Missions, who was one of those priests with Monseigneur Berneux in the Corea, who escaped when the Bishop, Henri Dorié, and others were all martyred. But she said he was only longing for permission to return there, for that the fervour of the Corean natives exceeded anything he had ever known in Europe. The good old priest of the mission came in as we were talking, and began mourning over the departure of the Duc and Duchesse de Magenta

(Maréchal and Madame Mac Mahon), who were, he said, the best and kindest people who had ever been placed at the head of affairs in Algeria. Afterwards, we had ample proof of this in other places, for they have left behind them a name which will never be effaced from the hearts of the people.

The smell of burning cedar was fragrant and strong through the whole town as we mounted our horses the following morning to start for the forest. Our cavalcade was a numerous one, as, in addition to the officers and ourselves, the maids accompanied us in a ' cacolet,' or seats fastened on each side of a big mule, and a sumpter mule with provisions, besides two or three Arab guides (who followed us as much for their own amusement as for our benefit), swelled the little cavalcade. The first portion of the road wound over barren hills, with only a few Arab tents here and there, and we had to make a great *détour* over some very rough tracks to avoid a ' dreary swindle swamp ' caused by the sudden melting of the snow. But soon we came to a beautiful ilex and cork wood, through which the path wound higher and higher amidst an underwood of fragrant and flowering shrubs ; with beautiful peeps of the distant mountains opening out here and there. No human habitation was to be seen ; but vast flocks of goats, and mountain sheep, and small dun and black and brown cattle, fed among the hills,

guarded by Arab boys wilder-looking than themselves.
The road became more and more precipitous, till we
were forced to dismount and lead our horses up the
steep and stony path through a fir wood, which every
moment got thicker and thicker. At last, after three
hours of this scrambling and struggling, we suddenly
emerged into an open meadow covered with snow, a
little beyond which was, the object of our expedition,—
the magnificent cedars of Teniet-el-Had. Though not
so large as some of those in the Lebanon range (the
average stems being from fifteen to eighteen feet in
circumference) they are far more numerous, and the
effect of the snow on their feathery branches sparkling
in the noonday sun was beautiful in the extreme. In
the very heart of the wood, on a little plateau cleared of
trees, is the picturesque Swiss chalet of the keeper of
the forest, who has a large room on one side for pic-nic
parties. But, unfortunately, he was not at home, so we
had to content ourselves with making a huge cedar-
wood fire outside the chalet, and spreading our
luncheon on some planks which we found lying in
plenty round the spot. The view from hence of the
Atlas Mountains beyond the forest was quite beautiful.
We were soon joined by our military acquaintances of
the night before, who had come on foot, having
attempted the regular road and finding the snow too
deep and yet too soft to bear their weight on horse-

back, had left their horses at a cantonnier's house about
two miles off, and walked the remainder of the way.
They strongly advised us, however, to brave the snow,
and to see the view from the upper path or terrace
over our heads, which was infinitely more extensive.
M —— refused ; but I could not resist the temptation,
and started with my escort, wading through the half-
melting, half-freezing snow, and continually sinking up
to my knees in the drifts, till we arrived at the top of
the glen from whence our little encampment by the
chalet looked like a distant speck.   Wet and weary as
I was, I must own that the panorama well repaid the
effort.   The whole double mountain ranges were
visible, the high peak of the Waransenis standing out
far above the rest, their snowy tops glistening in
the noon-day sun.   To the south, was the magnificent
plain and valley of the Chelif, which we had traversed the day before, with the fortress of Miliana
shining so brightly on the horizon (although eighty
miles off) that it seemed as if a short ride would bring
one to its gates.   Around and below us was the
beautiful foreground of cedars, with their dark green
foliage and red stems ; while here and there the snow
had melted and disclosed patches of the brightest,
tenderest spring verdure, amidst which snowdrops, a
dwarf blue iris, white jonquils, a purple gentian, and

pink hepaticæ blossomed brightly, as if defying the wintry blasts.

Our military friends were right : for, on the whole, I had never seen so striking or so magnificent a view. It reminded me the whole way of the Lebanon, and was similar both in character and vegetation. Later in the season, when the flowers and shrubs would be more fully out, it must be a perfect paradise. Still, what it must gain in one way it would lose in the other, for cedars never look so beautiful as in contrast with the snow. The descent of the mountain was more difficult as the ground froze under our feet, and defied any sure footing for man or beast. I was thoroughly drenched up to the waist by the time I returned to the chalet, where a roaring fire of cedar logs was fortunately crackling to dry and warm our half-frozen limbs. We returned to Teniet by a road so bad that we were again forcibly reminded of Syria! Luckily, our horses were quiet and sure-footed, and except that one of our party rolled into a mountain stream, we reached our little inn without accident.

The weather had been glorious all day, with a deliciously hot sun ; but towards evening the cold became intense, so that we were not sorry to huddle round the kitchen fire, and drink the hot coffee which our landlady had thoughtfully provided for us. There are some mineral springs close to the cedar forest,

E

which we did not go and see, but which are often
resorted to by the French soldiers after the intermittent
fevers so common in this country during the summer.
Dr. Bertherand has given a careful analysis of these
waters, which resemble in their qualities those of
Hamman-Meskhroutin, which we visited later, so that
I will not dwell upon those of Teniet. There is no
arrangement yet made for baths and no accommodation for bathers, so that the whole thing is in its infancy
at present.

On the following day we started again on horseback,
but in a contrary direction, to visit the ruined fortress of
Taza, one of the strongholds of Abd-el-Kader, perched
under the shadow of the mountain called Ech-Chaou,
which is between 5,000 and 6,000 feet above the level
of the sea. The road wound through beautiful gorges
and ravines, between mountains fringed with ilex, and
across bright rushing streams, which we had to wade
through every ten minutes, until M—— wearied of the
monotony of the road, suggested that we should give
up seeing the fortress, and turn into one of the little
valleys to the left which looked unusually tempting.
Leaving the beaten track, therefore, we rode up the
glen, following the course of the river, till we came
upon an open grassy space shaded by pine trees, close
to a large Arab encampment. After eating our
luncheon, we accepted the invitation of the Sheik to

visit his tent, which was pitched on a rising ground a
little above the river. The watch-dogs, as usual, barked
furiously; but restrained by their owners from tearing
us in pieces (as they otherwise would certainly have
done), we entered the long low black Bedouin home,
followed by a whole tribe of women and children, all
tattooed and nearly naked. Resting against the pole
in the centre were two little calves; a pet lamb was
tethered a little further off; while a quantity of cocks
and hens ran in and out or fluttered against our feet,
as if dismayed at our intrusion. One of the women
was weaving the striped brown and white canvas for
the tents as well as it could be done in any factory at
home, and on the same principle—the shuttle being
passed through the woof, which was stretched on
pulleys. The women had their eyes dyed with kohl
underneath, and had certain marks on the chin which
they told us were a sign of their tribe. One had a shell
round her neck as a charm; but all looked skinny,
ugly, and half starved. Large flocks of camels and
sheep were, however, herded by their children all
round the encampment; and they made us understand
that they were nomads, and should remove further
inland as soon as the grass was exhausted in the
present neighbourhood. Two of the grown-up sons
came in as we were speaking, fine handsome Arabs in
the Bedouin dress, who saluted us gravely and

courteously, and showed us their horses, which were tethered at the tent door. The women had all disappeared on the arrival of the men, though we saw them peeping at us under the canvas of one of the tents as we mounted to return home. We were given a great bowl of *kous-kous* for our dinner that evening; which is a sort of paste worked by the hand into a grain like semolina, and served either with sour milk or a greasy kind of soup : a most horrible composition to my mind, which no future experience could make me appreciate.

At five o'clock the following morning, we started on our return to Miliana in the same miserable convey-ance, and with the additional inconvenience of having a fifth passenger inside; the wife of the keeper of the forest. But at any rate, it was daylight, and we had had our night's rest; so that we were more fitted to cope with the fatigues and discomforts of the journey. We stopped to breakfast this time at another caravan-seray, which seemed built entirely for defence, with a square high wall and loop-holed windows. It was in a beautiful spot; the thuya, ilex and stone pines clothing all the hills around; while a profusion of cistus in full blossom, lentisk, juniper, filarea, squill and ferula (with its plume-like stalk of yellow bloom) formed a varied and beautiful underwood, over every bough of which the Algerian clematis, with its feathery bell-like flowers and pods, wreathed itself in a thousand fantastic shapes. We reached Miliana about five; the setting sun flooding the glorious plain below with crimson light, gilding the snowy tips of the hills with a soft rose colour, while, as usual, in the far distance, the grand peak of the Waransenis (the highest of the Atlas range), stood out sharply and clearly against the ruddy sky.

It was market day, and the Arabs were crowded together on the plain below the town; screaming and gesticulating as if each were furious with the other, but in reality only occupied in ordinary business trans-actions. We crossed the Chelif safely in the cart, though the water, this time, was above the horses' shoulders. This is the largest of the Algerian rivers; and both it and every other stream we passed were shaded with beautiful oleanders on both sides of the bank.

A bright hot sun streaming into our windows woke us early the following morning, and we went to enjoy a last view from the terrace before being cooped up again in the *coupé* of the diligence which was to take us to Bou-Medfa, on our way to Blidah. The pano-rama seemed more beautiful each time we gazed upon it; and it was with real regret that we turned away for the last time, and scrambled into our prison, which rapidly rolled through the gates and the plane-tree

avenue, and so on to the open country. The road
wound higher and higher, and at every turn we came
upon a fresh mountain or valley, each more beautiful
than the last, and richly wooded dells and vineyards—a
perfect picture of smiling plenty. At our feet, in front
of the low *coupé* where we sat, was a magnificent wild
boar, which had been killed in the mountains above
Miliana the day before, and was being sent as a
present to the Governor of Blidah. Just before reaching Bou-Medfa, we came to a picturesque 'koubba,'
one of the many tombs erected to a certain Sidi-Abd-
el-Kader, the patron of travellers and also of beggars,
judging by the numbers who invoke the aid of the
passers-by for the love of this their favourite saint.

At three o'clock the train started for Blidah, the line
running through the wild and beautiful rocky valley of
La Chiffa, and then emerging into the great Metidja
Plain up to the little smiling, orange-shaded town,
which the Arabs call the 'Rose' of Algeria. We
found very comfortable rooms in the Hôtel d'Orient,
looking on the little arcaded 'Place;' and I went out
to find the church, (which is quite beautiful, being an old
mosque converted into a church,) where I found both
Exposition and Benediction.

After breakfast the next day, we started for the
gorge of La Chiffa, stopping on the way just outside
the town at the 'Sacred Wood,' which was revered

even in Roman times, and is now equally so by the
Arabs. In it are olive trees as old as those in the
garden of Gethsemane. In the centre of the wood are
two 'koubbas,' one of great note, which was richly
decorated, hung with silks and stuffs of gold and silver,
lit with innumerable tapers and sweet with incense.
Whilst we were there, an Arab gentleman brought his
little boy to the marabout (or priest), who was sitting on
a mat at the door, and they recited alternately some
prayers; after which the boy presented his offering—
a wax candle and a small piece of money, and kissed
the marabout's hand. Then two women followed, all
in white, as usual, like spectres, completely covered in
their haïks, with only one eye showing. We found they
were a lady and her maid; and when they entered the
chapel, I saw that the lady was richly dressed, with
beautiful gold coins round her neck and arms, and that
her 'haïk' was fastened with gold brooches or clasps
curiously wrought and connected with a chain. The
maid brought out from under her burnous, a piece of
fine muslin for a gown, and laid it on the tomb—where
it was sprinkled by the marabout three times with
holy water, and thus evidently consecrated for use.
I thought it touching, that sanctifying of an every-day
object before making it up; and the way in which the
lady prayed made one feel she was in earnest, and that
God would hear her, however mistaken the poor soul's

faith might be. The garden was full of mimosa in full bloom, and other flowering shrubs. The magnolias also were fully out, while the borders were divided by dwarf China roses, cut into low hedges. Then we went on to La Chiffa, the road crossing a wooden bridge, passing by a convict soldiers' prison (where the men were employed in a rope-yard), and then, turning sharply to the left, wound higher and higher, up a narrow gorge, through beautifully and richly wooded hills, with a rushing torrent beneath, very like the pass of the St. Gothard, until we came to a grotto, which we entered ; and found it full of stalactites and petrified aloes, which had retained their soft green colour. Beautiful maidenhair fern grew out of every crevice of the rocks, moistened by the dripping of the spring, which burst forth on every side. A little further on, to the right, we came to a half-way house where a large eagle had just been killed, a male bird, measuring a great size from wing to wing. This part of the gorge is called ' La Vallée des Singes,' and we soon saw a couple of tailless monkeys scrambling over the rocks, which abounded in natural cascades, and swinging themselves joyously from the branches above the falls. The old lady at the café grumbled dreadfully at them, and taking us to see her garden, exclaimed : ' Ah ! ces coquins, ils me mangent tout !' After resting, and feeding the horses, we went on again till we came to

another bridge at the junction of two rivers, the Oued-
Merja, and the Chiffa, which is nearly at the top of the
pass. Here are extensive iron and copper mines, and
a little colony of miners; and from hence the road
branches off to Médéah, a French military station,
built on the ruins of a Roman town, of which an
aqueduct and certain Latin inscriptions still remain;
and forming one of that chain of forts whereby the
French have secured the comparatively peaceful occupation of their Algerian provinces. The descent of the
pass, on our return to Blidah, was even more beautiful
than the ascent, as the plain of the Metidja appeared
through the narrow and precipitous gorge like a sunny,
smiling picture in a dark rugged frame—the sun
lighting up the sea on the horizon in a bright line of
silvery light.

In coming back, we made a *détour* of the town to
visit the famous orange groves, which are simply
fabulous for beauty and number. I had seen them in
Spain, at Cintra, at Mentone, at Mola di Gaetà, in Sicily
—but nothing approached the wonderful luxuriance
of the Blidah Gardens. There are millions of oranges
and citrons of every sort, and of every size, and
flavour. We stopped at one of the gardens and
went in to eat, calling upon the proprietor, who lived
in a little house in the centre of the wood. He told
us that his orange grove had not been planted longer

than ten or twelve years, and that it was enough to
stick a shoot in the ground to make it grow: that
the oranges were worth fifteen francs the thousand if
not sorted; and if carefully picked, twenty-five francs
the thousand. The alleys were bordered with Neapolitan violets of immense size, of which we gathered
great bunches which scented the whole air. The
owner of the garden loaded us with mandarins for
our journey, and would accept of no payment for that
which in fact was spoiling under the trees for want
of gatherers. How I longed to turn some of our
English school children into those fragrant shady
groves!

From the orange gardens we went to the 'Haras'
of Arab horses, belonging to the French Government.
There are one or two very fine stallions of pure
Arab breed, and some good shaped mares, though
with the usual fault of being too long in the pastern.
But we were told that the greater number of the
horses had been sacrificed to the exigencies of the
war. Some beautiful little gazelles were feeding in
the paddocks, which had been captured by the officers
in the interior.

In the evening I went to see the Sisters of the
'Doctrine Chrétienne.' They have not been molested
here by the Revolutionary Government; but are
universally beloved, and have the only 'pension' in

the place for girls of the upper classes; besides the
national or poor schools, which number upwards of
500 children. There are nineteen sisters, and a very
cheery bright-looking superior, Ma Sœur Paul, whose
very face did one good to see.

The following day we left Blidah for Algiers. It
certainly is the most attractive little place I ever saw,
situated at the foot of the Atlas range, and combining
beautiful mountain scenery and delicious walks and
rides, with the most luxuriant vegetation and the
freshest streams. House rent is low and living cheap,
while the climate is everything that can be desired.
The only *revers de la médaille* is, that it is subject to
earthquakes, one of which, only a few years ago,
destroyed all the principal buildings in the great
square; in spite of which the inhabitants go on
building immensely high houses, with the same in-
fatuation and less reason than the inhabitants of
Torre del Greco; who cluster round the very base of
the volcano which has so often destroyed their homes.

At eight o'clock that evening we reached Algiers
by the new railroad, and found comfortable rooms,
looking on the sea, ready for us at the Hôtel d'Orient.
I never saw anything so beautiful as the effect of the
town by night as we approached it. The line from
the Maison Carrée (about seven miles off) runs along

the sea shore, and Algiers with its brilliant masses of white houses glistening in the moonlight, and the multitude of gas lights at different heights dotted upon the hill side and reflected in the water, looked like a succession of hanging stars against the dark clear sky.

ALGERIAN CUPBOARD, IN RECESS, WITH POTTERY

NEW ALGIERS

CHAPTER III.

ALGIERS.

EVERYONE who knows anything of this place, however superficially, is aware that it is now divided into two distinct towns— the French, with its broad streets, boulevards, and Rue de Rivoli-looking houses, and the Arab, with its steep narrow passages (which are rather like a succession of dark, dirty staircases,) its beautiful doorways, from which glimpses may be obtained of exquisite Moorish courts inside, its picturesque fountains and mosques, its crowded bazaars and all the appearances of Oriental life. In proportion as the French town encroaches on the other, the beauty and interest of Algiers are lost; and this applies equally to Constantine, which has preserved far more than Algiers, the 'cachet Arabe.' I think I had better describe the place exactly as we saw it, and leave my readers to draw their own conclusions.

I should premise that we arrived at a moment of

transition and almost of revolution. There had been half-a-dozen different governments in as many weeks, who were only agreed in two things—the destruction of religious education, and the promotion of the Jews to places of honour in the council and the army ; the fatal effects of which changes we remained at Algiers long enough to witness. The Archbishop was away : having prudently remained in France till the storm had passed over, so as to avoid coming into direct and inevitable collision with the existing authorities.

Our first visit was to the Cathedral, which was formerly a mosque, and has a fine façade, of three arched doorways, crowned by two towers ; a handsome flight of twenty steps leading up to the main entrance. The interior consists of a series of sculptured arches in the Moorish style, resting on marble columns, the old Koran texts, in gold letters on a red or black ground, still remaining round the cupola over the high altar. To the right, on entering the church, is the marble monument of the martyr Geronimo, who was put to death in the fifteenth century for the faith of Christ, by being buried alive in the mortar of the fort called 'Des Vingt-Quatre Heures' which was then in process of construction. His body was discovered and solemnly translated to the cathedral on December 27, 1853; the two marble angels, carved on either side of the tomb, seeming to be watching for the moment of his glorious resurrection. The people have a great devotion to this venerable martyr, and his chapel is rarely deserted.

The Archbishop's palace is directly opposite the cathedral, and is a beautiful specimen of an old Moorish house. There is the open court, surrounded with graceful arcades, supporting the gallery above, with its marble columns, and exquisitely carved horse-shoe arches, leading into all the principal rooms, of which the ceilings and walls are a marvel of plastic art; while the doors, generally of cedar wood, are carved in wonderful Arabesque devices, and the lower portions of the rooms and passages are inlaid with highly glazed encaustic tiles of the most beautiful colours and patterns. The only difference in these Moorish houses, is in the amount of carving and decoration in each house; but the plan of them all is the same; so that this description equally applies to the Governor's house to the right of the cathedral, although of course, the reception rooms are larger; and the court is full of beautiful palms and exotics.

Afterwards, we went up the hill to that part of Algiers, called 'Mustapha Supérieur,' where the most beautiful villas and summer residences of the inhabitants are situated, to call upon the English Consul, Colonel Lyon Playfair. He was most kind and good-natured and volunteered to take us to see a wonderful old

Moorish house, near his own, called the ' Hydra,' which has lately been bought by the famous chess-player, M. de St.-Armand. Its arrangements were perfect: with the outer court for those who wait, the inner court or quadrangle surrounded with horse-shoe arches and twisted marble pillars (three at the corners and two at the sides) and the same above; a gallery running round the two upper stories, into which all the living rooms opened, and the whole surmounted by a flat terrace, from which there is a glorious view. Every room is fitted up with carved and coloured wood work, in the Moorish style—beds, cupboards, chairs, &c. and with Moorish or Kabyle pottery and lamps. All the floors and walls were tiled with those beautiful old Spanish tiles, the art of making which seems now extinct. In each room, too, were those curious depressed arches which are found only in Algiers.

The lady of the house was a most curious old woman, who had been a *vivandière*, but was very good-natured, and gave us a beautiful nosegay of roses. She was very proud of her beautiful old house, and yet lived entirely in the kitchen, among her cocks and hens.

We returned by the Kasba, or old Arab fort, of which the walls and turrets alone remain. At every turn we came upon picturesque ' koubbas ' or mosques, shaded with palms; and groups of Arabs or Moors, mingled with negresses in their blue-striped burnouses, or Jewesses with their black head-dresses—an infinite variety of costumes which would delight the heart of a painter.

Our next visit was to the museum and library, which we reached by climbing up a narrow street, called la Rue Lothopage, and up a succession of those long low steps, known by the Italians as *gradini*, to a very handsome doorway, which admitted us into a species of vestibule, with arcades and columns, and a marble seat running round it, from whence we entered into the quadrangle, or court of one of the most beautiful Moorish houses in Algiers. There were the same horse-shoe arches, and twisted columns, and galleries, and coloured tiles, as at the Archbishop's palace; only the woodwork of the galleries was more finely carved, the doors and ceilings were of more elaborate patterns, and the stonework looked like the most delicate guipure lace. The curator of the library, which was opened in 1838, is a Mr. McHardy, a very clever, agreeable man, who, most good-naturedly, took us over the whole place, and showed us everything that was most curious and interesting. The first thing which struck me on coming in was a life-size cast of the martyr Geronimo, just as he lay in the fort. His body, which was found intact, had left a complete

mould, into which plaster had been run, and the
result is a full-length figure with its face downwards
and the hands tied behind the back. There is no
expression of pain in the face, which is of Kabyle
type, but the hands are clenched inwards as if in
agony.

There were a number of Roman statues, Mosaic
pavements, and early Christian sarcophagi and inscriptions in this museum, besides a multitude of Roman
and Pagan sculptures, and some beautiful pillars in
Oriental alabaster. They have been collected from
Cherchel, Tlemcen, and various other parts of Algeria ;
but although it is interesting to see them all together,
it was impossible not to regret their being removed
from the localities where they were found, and where
their historical interest would have been doubled.

In the library are some valuable illuminated editions
of the Koran, especially one of the fourteenth and
another of the sixteenth century. The illuminations
are quite exquisite, and far surpass any I ever saw in
our missals as to finish and delicacy of design, although,
of course, no figures are introduced, they being contrary to the Mahometan law. The Spanish Korans
were written in the Cufic, the others in the Arabic
character, and the binding of one of them was the
most beautiful specimen of tooled work possible. The
paper on which these illuminations are done is of a

peculiar kind, and made only in Constantinople; they
never used vellum for copies of the Koran.   Mr.
McHardy then took us up to the terrace and into his
own rooms, which are full of curious little alcoves, and
Moorish arches, and coloured tiles.   He showed us a
machine for taking astronomical observations, of which
there are only **three** others known, one at Vienna, one
in Paris, and one in our British Museum ; but this one
is the most complicated and curious.   It is of the
thirteenth century.   The house itself, which is worthy
of the treasures it contains, was built at the end of the
fourteenth century.   But every old house in Algiers is
beautiful, and especially every old doorway and door.

In the evening we drove to the ' Jardin d'Essai,' or
botanical garden, which is full of scarce and valuable
plants and shrubs, with a magnificent avenue of date
and fan palms stretching down to the sea : while
another was formed of bamboos, meeting overhead
almost like those of Trinidad.   One portion of the
ground is planted with bread fruit and plantains,
another with oranges and citrons ; but it was too early
in the year for many flowers. Some beautiful peacocks
were sunning themselves on the terrace, and opposite
the entrance gate is the dome of a circular ' Koubba '
or tomb of a saint supposed to be capable of bilocation,
whence named *Bou-Kobrin*.   It is a very picturesque
spot surrounded by olive and lentisk trees and magni-

ficent aloes and cactuses, and is a great place of
pilgrimage on Fridays, when the Moslem women all
come to pray on the tombs of the departed. A beautiful Arab fountain a little further on adjoins the 'Café
des Platanes,' a favourite resort of the Algerians on
fête days, which did not surprise us; for, shaded as it
is by magnificent plane trees, and with the constant
cool trickling of the water, and the picturesque
ever-varying groups of camels, horses and donkeys
which, with their Arab or negro drivers, invariably
stopped here to drink on their way to and from the
city, the spot had a sort of fascination for me,
especially after the glare and heat and dust of the
road beyond.

Another half-hour's drive brought us to a village
called Koubba, at the top of a steep hill, overlooking
the whole bay as far as Cape Matifou. Here is a large
seminary for priests, and a college for such of the Arab
boys collected during the famine as displayed a taste
for reading or literary pursuits. A venerable old man
showed me all over the buildings and church, which is
only half finished; but its large white dome or cupola
is quite a landmark in the country. Hard by, is a large
orphanage for girls called 'La Sainte Enfance,' which
we had not time to visit. We came home by a very
picturesque and beautifully wooded gorge called 'De
la Femne sauvage,' leading to the pretty village of

' le Ruisseau ; ' but there is endless beauty and variety
in the drives and rides round Algiers.

The next day we paused in our sight-seeing to go
with Madame de C—— and her beautiful daughter
to see a Jewish wedding, for which she had kindly
obtained us an invitation. We were received in an
alcoved room, where a breakfast of sweetmeats, cakes,
and sweet wines was set out, the bride and her
parents being seated on a divan at one end, dressed in
rich Jewish costume. After a short time, we were told
to precede the young lady to the Moorish vapour bath,
which is the next part of the ceremony. Such a marvellous scene as there met our eye I despair of repro-
ducing on paper! About fifty young Jewish girls,
from twelve to twenty years of age, whose only clothing was a scarf of gold or silver gauze round their loins,
with their beautiful dark hair all down their backs, and
their lovely white necks and arms covered with necklaces and bracelets, were seen dimly standing in the
water through a cloud of steam and incense, waiting
for the bride, and when she appeared received her
with loud shrill cries of ' Li ! Li ! Li !' in a continually
ascending scale. Amongst these girls were hideous
negresses equally scantily clothed, and one or two of
them with their black woolly hair dyed bright orange
colour : these were the bathing-women. They seized
us by the arm and wanted to force us to undress too,

which we stoutly resisted; and took refuge on the raised marble slab which surrounded the bath, and where the pretty little bride, with her mother and aunts, was standing waiting to be unrobed too. They took off her heavy velvet clothes, and she appeared in a beautiful gold-figured gauze chemise and some lovely short red and gold drawers; they then led her, with the same cries, into an inner room, which was stifling with wet vapour and steam, and here the poor child, who was only thirteen, remained for three mortal hours, the women pouring water on her head from picturesque-shaped gold jars, and every kind of cosmetic and sweet scent being rubbed upon her. Being unable to stand the intense heat and overpowering smell any longer, we escaped for a time into the open air; but returned after about an hour, to find another bride going through the same ceremonies. Some of the bridesmaids were very beautiful; one especially, though a Jewess, had regularly *golden* hair and blue eyes. And the whole scene was like a ballet at the opera, or rather a set of naiads or water nymphs in a picture; not like anything in real life! Their glorious hair floating over their shoulders, with their beautifully modelled arms rounded in graceful curves as they disported themselves round the bride, would have driven a sculptor or painter wild with delight! But I could not get over the indelicacy of the whole

thing : it was *a scene in the nude* with a vengeance !
A heavy curtain was hung over the outer courts of the
bath room, where a quantity of Arabs were clustered.
Madame de C—— told me that this was the only
chance the men had of seeing their future wives, who
purposely let a little corner of their veils or haiks drop
as they came out, under pretence of their being brushed
aside by the curtain.

At half-past three o'clock the following morning, we
got up and went to the bride's house for the conclusion
of the ceremony. A great crowd of men and musicians
were grouped in the lower court. Above, the bride
was sitting in state, in the deep recess of a handsome
Moresque room, veiled in white gauze, while a red and
gold figured scarf hung in graceful folds behind her
head. On either side of her were two venerable-looking old men with long white beards, and in front of her,
another, holding a candelabrum with three candles.
They were Rabbis, and chanted psalms alternately
with songs of praise about ' the dove with the beautiful
eyes,' &c. ; in fact, a sort of canticle. All this time,
the minstrels in the quadrangle below were ' making a
noise,' while over the carved gallery above, looking
down upon them, leant a variety of Jewish women, all
beautifully dressed in brown velvet and satin, with
stomachers and girdles richly brocaded in gold and
gold-embroidered lappets hanging from the black silk

headdress which is the invariable costume of their race. This went on *for hours*, till the poor little bride looked quite worn out. From time to time spoonfuls of soup were put into her mouth, which she strove to resist; and then she was conducted into the court below, where the same ceremonies were gone through, except that a species of buffoon danced before her, and was rewarded by ten-franc bits put into his mouth, which he kept in his cheek while drawling out a queer kind of song, which we supposed was witty, as the audience were in fits of laughter. Everything was done, both upstairs and down, to make the bride laugh, even to chucking and pulling her under the chin! But she remained impassive, it being part of her business to look grave, and to prove by her demureness that she was old enough to be married. All of a sudden, the same unearthly cry or yell of ' Li! Li! Li!' was heard in the outside court, caught up instantly by everyone in and out of the house. I thought of the words, ' Behold the bridegroom cometh!' so exactly were the old traditions preserved. A very ordinary-looking youth in a frock coat and red fez accordingly made his appearance, and then the women covered their faces with their gauze handkerchiefs, and the men, who had never ceased eating and drinking at intervals during the whole night, formed themselves into a procession; while the bride's father (a venerable looking old Jew, with a

long white beard, white turban and crimson sash) led
her to the carriage which was to take her to the bridegroom's home, we all following, and the women's cry
of 'Li! Li! Li! Li!' resounding through the narrow
streets.

Getting into our carriages, we accompanied her to
St. Eugène, about a mile from the town, and there left
her, just as the day dawned, after all her fatigues, to the
(we will hope) peaceful enjoyment of her new home.

We resolved to devote the next day to visiting the
principal mosques of Algiers, and for this purpose took
with us 'Mahmoud,' the interpreter of the hotel, as we
were rather afraid of venturing into Mahometan
sanctuaries alone. He took us first to *Djama Kebir,*
the oldest mosque in Algiers, having been finished in
the tenth century of the Christian era and in the year
400 of the Hegira. The approach to it is by a series
of beautiful arcades resting on white marble pillars,
and leading into a large open court shaded by orange-
trees, in the centre of which is a most picturesque
fountain. The mosque itself is very large and very
dark inside, with a perfect forest of marble pillars
and curiously indented arches forming a succession of
aisles, with the usual 'mihrab' or pulpit.[1] A famous
Marabout was about to preach, whom Mahmoud
informed us was the *archbishop* of the Maléki, or that

[1] See Frontispiece.

sect among the Mahometans which was the most popular among the Arabs and Moors in Algiers. But as he evidently did not wish us to remain for the great man's sermon (which would certainly have been utterly unintelligible to us), we went on to the exhibition of national manufactures and products, which is held in a building near the Admiralty and almost adjoining the mosque. It was a very interesting collection, pleasantly and well arranged, and reflects great credit on the authorities. Here were exposed every kind of marble and metal found in Algeria ; every description of wood, including the beautiful *thuya*, like a dark reddish cedar ; every sort of manufacture, from the delicate transparent ' haïk ' to the beautiful carpets of Llarouat, with saddlery, leather-work, arms, and jewellery ; besides beasts and birds, flowers and fruit, fossils and minerals, shells and corals, butterflies and insects ; in fact, all those riches, animal, vegetable, and mineral, which, if properly *exploité*, would make Algeria the most valuable colony in the world.

From the exhibition we drove to the picturesque gardens of Marengo, passing by the fort called ' Des Vingt-quatre Heures,' where Geronimo was buried alive. At the end of a beautiful avenue stands the mosque and Arab cemetery of *Abd-er-Rhaman-et-Tcalbi*, a saint who lived in the fourteenth century, and who is so much venerated by the Mahometans that all

the pashas and great functionaries strive to be buried
near his tomb or 'koubba,' which is most richly and
beautifully decorated. The minaret of this mosque is
the most graceful in Algiers, as also the carved portico,
which is shaded by fine palms. The doorways are
beautifully carved, as also the mihrab; and the tiles are
of the most varied and brilliant patterns. Ahmed,
Bey of Constantine, is likewise buried here; he was as
cruel as he was treacherous, and though they showed us
a chain which he had caused to be severed off the leg of
a captive, and which weighed no one knows how many
hundred-weight, yet we also saw his bastinado, a cord
thick enough to kill a man with four or five blows,
with a huge blood-stained ball at the end! It was
Friday, and women clothed in white from head to foot
were flitting about like spectres from tomb to tomb,
strewing green myrtle and yellow jonquils on the
graves, on which they likewise offered broth, wine, and
bread. To judge by their absorption, poor souls, their
prayers must undoubtedly have been in earnest; and
one poor mother, weeping over the tomb of her only
boy, which she had covered with flowers, touched me
very much.

From this beautiful spot we toiled up towards the
Kasba, and saw there a very primitive old mosque,
without any ornament save some fine ancient marble
pillars; and then wandered through the narrow, steep,

dirty streets, with their projecting wooden buttresses, casting sharp shadows on the white walls below, till we reached the Dey's house, the palace of that last Dey of Algiers, whose box in the ear to the French Consul cost him his throne, and gave Algiers to France. A small mosque opposite the gates of the palace remains, which has been turned into a Catholic chapel and school. There is a large chain which hangs before the entrance gate, to which, if a criminal flies and clings, he is safe from the pursuit of justice. Leaving the Kasba, which has been turned into a barrack, we crept down through the picturesque narrow streets, with their beautiful archways and Toledo-nailed doors, till we came to an *ouvroir* for 120 Arab girls, under the care of a Mdme. Barroil. Their work is quite beautiful ; it is not embroidery, but useful white work for trousseaux, baby linen, &c. Then we went on to Madame Luce's Arab school, where a multitude of young Arab women and children are employed on the most exquisite embroidery. No attempt is made in either of these institutions to give the girls any religious instruction. They are solely intended to raise their moral tone, and enable them to earn their own living respectably. I ordered two ball dresses of Madame Luce, which were executed by these children with wonderful beauty and rapidity. They also embroider every kind of handkerchief and scarf, and that

in the greatest perfection, there being no *wrong* side
to their work, which therefore can be worn in any
way.

Then we poked about in queer old shops and
bazaars, buying Kabyle pots, and gold-woven scarfs,
and an illuminated impression of Mahomet's foot, &c. ;
after which we went to a regular *café maure*, and had
some real Turkish coffee, squatted on the matted stone
slabs which surrounded the room, and fancying ourselves again in Syria.

On our way down we saw another mosque, with the
same beautiful arches and pillars, and as full as it could
be of men and women praying ; and also looked
into the synagogue, which has lately been restored,
and contains some beautiful carved woodwork in the
screen which divides the Jewish women from the male
portion of the congregation. I have said before how
varied and beautiful the drives and rides are in the
same neighbourhood of Algiers, and, thanks to the
kindness of Lady L——— T———, whose pretty Moorish
villa is one of the sights of Mustapha Supérieur, we
were able to visit the greater portion of these spots,
and that under the pleasantest auspices. The first
day Lady L——— took us to Bou Zarea by a beautiful
road, and so on to the picturesque koubba of Sidi
Nouman, about a mile above the village, from whence
there is a magnificent view. The tomb is shaded by

fan palms, which here are allowed to grow to their full
proportions, forming graceful tufts of dark foliage
above the white cupola, which covers the remains of
the saint. Coming home we stopped to get some rare
varieties of fern in a lovely ravine close to a deserted
villa, of which the garden was full of roses and
Egyptian jessamine. The road then turned into
another valley called the 'Trois Vallons,' which is a
beautiful gorge on the St. Eugène side of the town,
ending in a narrow, circuitous path leading to the
much-frequented 'koubba' of Sidi-Medjber, which
boasts of a wonderful spring much resorted to by
Mahometan women, and which is situated in a perfect
thicket of orange, citron, pomegranate, almond and fig
trees. A rapid stream runs by the side of the road,
which in winter becomes a torrent, and overflows its
banks. The constant crumbling away of the banks
from the nature of the soil, and the consequent destruction of the roads in Algiers, is the despair of the
French engineers as well as of the inhabitants of these
picturesque valleys, as they are never quite sure
whether their houses may not be inaccessible before
morning; or even if, when they go into the town in
their carriages, they may be able to return!

Jewish tombs of a curious raised lozenge-shape were
scattered here and there on the hill side. A little
lower down is another valley, called 'De la Carrière,'

as it leads to a quarry from whence most of the stone has been extracted for the new buildings in and near Algiers. This road is very wooded and pretty, with little villas and Moorish houses peeping out among aloes and palms, and a rapid stream rushing below.

We were anxious, whilst in Algeria, to see all we could of the customs peculiar to the different nationalities which so greatly contribute to the interest and picturesqueness of the country; and accordingly, one Wednesday morning, started early for a grotto by the sea-shore, which, from time immemorial, has been devoted to what is called the 'negresses' sacrifice.' This grotto is situated on the road to St. Eugène, and, early as it was, we passed a number of women and children, on foot or on mules, all wending their way in the same direction, followed by servants carrying under their arms or in baskets a quantity of black or white fowls. When we arrived at the spot indicated by our driver, and had got out of the carriage, we discovered a flight of steep steps cut in the rock, leading down to a path by the seashore. This path turned suddenly to the right behind the projecting cliff and disclosed a semicircular cave, behind which was a spring called *Sebâ-Aïoun,* or the Seven Fountains. In the centre of this cave sat an old negress, ugly as a demon, dressed in a white turban and a great scarlet cloak; while, before her, a circular space was traced in the sand, in the centre of which was a kind of rude stove on which simmered various little earthenware pots of incense and benzoin. Presently an Arab lady came up, crying bitterly, saying ' that her husband had ceased to love her, and had taken a fancy to some one else.' She took from her maid two white and two black hens, which she presented to the negress, who first incensed both her and the fowls, then swung the birds by the legs three times over the lady's head, and all about her, and then slowly and only partially cut their throats, letting the blood flow into a little metal basin, with which she anointed the patient's hands and feet, between the eyes and on the forehead, all the while reciting prayers or rather incantations, the lady crossing her hands backwards and forwards in token of submission. The wretched birds were only half killed, and by the way they fluttered it was decided whether the charm had or had not been successful. If they fluttered towards the sea it was considered all right, and the negresses set up a shrill ' Li ! Li !' of triumph. If, on the other hand, the unhappy fowls struggled, in their death-agonies, towards the rock, the charm had failed, and the whole thing had to be done over again. Then the patient was made to drink of the spring and to wash in it three times, while she was again incensed by the negress. The same thing was repeated for each patient as he or she came up to the negress' cauldron, until the sand was strewed with dying fowls and blood, to a degree which was positively sickening. Other negresses were in attendance on the principal *guezzanates* as they are called, dressed in the blue check haïk of their race, and all equally revolting in manner and appearance. This sacrifice dates from the early Roman times, and is in fact a remnant of the old Pagan superstitions. The curious and painful thing to me was that, not only Jewesses but even French Christians came to be cured and submitted to all these horrible rites and incantations. I spoke to one woman whom I had seen in the morning at the Cathedral, and asked her ' how she could reconcile it to her conscience to seek relief in such a manner ? ' She replied : ' I believe in the cures effected by these negresses; and if theirs is a bad agency, at any rate it is overruled for good. God is in heaven and we on earth, and He can bless whatever means we use.'

This woman had brought her little boy, who was suffering from fever, and the negresses bedaubed the poor child all over with blood, which made him cry bitterly. I turned away in disgust, thinking the whole thing horribly heathenish and cruel ; and marvelling that any Christian mother should thus like to risk the fate of her child.

This was the first day of the great Arab feast of Baïram, and every family who could afford it killed a lamb or a sheep on the occasion. But in the evening there was a rising of the Arabs against the Jews which nearly produced serious results. It arose from the folly of the Government in appointing a Jew as judge of an Arab court, and still more in enrolling a regiment of Jews as Francs-tireurs.

Now the Arabs loathe and despise the Jews more than any nation upon earth; so that to be judged by them, and to see the Jews in possession of arms, which had been denied to themselves, was the height of insult towards the whole Moslem race and the most impolitic act of which the French authorities could possibly be guilty. The ill-usage of an Arab boy, condemned by this very judge, fanned the flame; and towards four or five o'clock, a multitude of Arabs armed with long sticks, met in the principal square and began destroying all the Jewish stalls they could find. The Chief Justice, M. Pierrey, a French gentleman much and justly beloved by the Arabs for his kindness and impartiality, endeavoured to calm the tumult, but an accidental blow from a stone laid him low and the intervention of the military at last became necessary. A great many arrests were the consequence; but the Arabs in reality gained their object; for the Government took fright, disbanded the Jewish regiment, and removed the obnoxious judge; so that tranquillity was at last restored.

A few evenings later, we went to see another religious ceremony, but this time one performed by a peculiar sect among the Arabs, in memory of a holy marabout, who, being lost in the desert, with his followers, is supposed to have obtained the power from God of turning scorpions, snakes, and cactus leaves into wholesome food, and thereby was saved with his disciples from perishing with hunger. This festival is called the *Aïoussa*, and we had been warned that we should be horrified at parts of the performance; however, we were determined to see everything, and so at nine o'clock in the evening started with a party of friends, on foot, up the narrow, dark steep Arab streets till we reached a court near the Kasba from whence already issued sounds of tum-tums, tambourines and other kinds of Arab music. Passing through a low door, we came into a Moorish house, of which the lower court was filled on one side with musicians, while the marabouts or priests of this peculiar sect, sat in a solemn half circle on the other. It was dark, except that in the centre of the court a fire was burning; and round the gallery above, were massed all the women of the establishment, closely shrouded in their haïks, it is true, but quite as much excited as the men. Coffee was handed round; and after that was over, we were grouped on one side of the court and the performance began by the musicians playing on their tambourines, and gradually increasing in speed, while two men came forward and danced, very much like the Dervishes we had seen at Cairo. After a few moments, they retired and then came back again, getting more and more excited every moment till they began to leap furiously into the air, to growl like angry camels, to eat great mouthfuls of snakes, scorpions, and prickly cactus-leaves ; and, in fact, to behave like brute beasts, or like men possessed of evil spirits. After a time, these two withdrew, and two others took their place and commenced by putting bars of metal into the furnace till they were red hot ; and then, bending them with their hands, they began to burn the soles of their feet and other parts of their bodies ; the smell of the singeing flesh adding to the horror of the scene.

I stole up from the court below to the gallery above; and there found that the women were almost wild with delight, screaming in unison with the men, dancing and swaying their bodies to and fro, clapping their hands and making frantic demonstrations of pleasure. Between each performance, the actors went up to the white-haired, long-bearded marabout in the centre of the circle and kissed his hand ; and the same ceremony was repeated before each scene was begun, when the marabout solemnly blessed the performers. Then

came the most disgusting part of the whole : when the
men, half naked, stood and knelt on the sharp edge of
a sword held by two others, the blade being turned
upwards ; and then poked pointed metal skewers
through their cheeks and tongues, and even into their
eyeballs ; the dancers waxing more and more furious
every moment, as well as the screaming and gesticulating of the actors and the ever-increasing noise of the
tambourines and tum-tums ; in fact, all this fearful din
combined with the semi-darkness, the smoke, the
smells, and the dense crowd, gave one more the idea
of the infernal regions than anything Dante ever wrote
or imagined! The whole scene was certainly most
wild and curious, but, to my mind, horrible; and all the
more when one reflects that 'Aïssa' is the name of our
Blessed Lord, and that this frightful sacrifice is supposed to be pleasing to Him! I felt a positive remorse
at having paid anything to encourage or perpetuate
such an exhibition, and all the more when I was told
that the greater part of the men were in hospital afterwards, and that we had only seen the mildest portion
of the performance! It was a real relief when we got
out of the house into the pure night air, and walked
home through the silent streets in the glorious moonlight, the quiet and calm of which were inexpressibly
refreshing after the two or three hours of mad excite-
ment we had witnessed.

I have only yet alluded slightly to that which makes one of the great charms of Algiers. I mean the picturesqueness and variety of the costumes, especially in the old town. At first, it was impossible to distinguish the different nationalities of the wearers. But by degrees we learnt to tell them almost at first sight.

The most picturesque are the Arabs *pur et simple*, with their tall erect figures, straight features, magnificent carriage, and dark eyes. There is one peculiarity about them, and that is that they *always* have their heads *covered*, the white headdress or capote of their burnouses being bound round the head with a thick cord of camels' hair wound round six or seven times. Their wives are shrouded from head to foot in white haïks and burnouses, the only sign of difference of rank being shown in the exceeding fineness of the stuff worn by the ladies which covers them completely, only one eye being allowed to be shown. These poor women are looked upon as beasts of burden in the tents and among the lower classes ; while among the upper, they are simply pampered slaves, whose one idea in life is to minister to the pleasure of their lords. Various attempts have been made by the French to emancipate them from this unhappy condition ; but, as yet, in vain. On this subject M. Cherbonneau (the Head of the Arabic French School and a learned archæologist, with whose labours we afterwards became better acquainted at Constantine) tells the following anecdote, which was related to him by the famous Mussulman lawyer, Si Chadli :—

A chief of the tribe of Haracta, between Aïn-Beïda and Tebessa, went on some business to Constantine. A few days later, he returned to his tribe and calling his wife, desired her to fetch four posts and some cord. She obeyed : when, to her horror, the chief threw her down on the ground, lashed her to the four stakes, and taking a stick commenced beating her with all his might. Her cries brought all the inhabitants of the tents to their doors, and one endeavoured, though in vain, to stop her husband's arm. 'But what has she done ?' they exclaimed. 'She is the pearl of the tribe, the best of mothers, the model of wives !' 'What has she done ?' retorted the monster. 'Nothing. I am only relieving my mind.' At last, being exhausted by his own fury, he condescended to stop and explain that at Constantine, he had seen an Arab woman, backed up by the French authorities, drag her husband before the court to complain of his ill-usage, and the Kadi had actually given judgment in *her* favour ! So monstrous an infraction of Arab usages had infuriated the chief to such a degree that he had forgotten the object of his journey, and only hurried home to wreak his vengeance

for the insult offered to the male sex, on the body of
his unhappy wife!

The Moors, unlike the Othellos of our childish
fancy, are simply Arabs who live in towns and have
intermarried with other races. They have the same
straight features, oval faces, and clear brown skins, only
a good deal fairer than the nomad Arab. But their
dress is different. They wear a turban or piece of
white muslin wound round a little red *shashea* or skull
cap, a jacket of bright-coloured cloth and two waist-
coats richly embroidered, full trousers, bare legs, and
large loose shoes. The dress of their women out of
doors is the haïk of their Arab sisters; but indoors
they wear a gauze chemise with short sleeves, wide
trousers, bare legs, and yellow *babouches* or slippers.
Their beautiful black hair is simply knotted behind the
head, while a little velvet *shashea*, richly embroidered,
is placed coquettishly on one side. A kind of vest of
the same material is sometimes added to define the
shape; and all have beautiful jewels, fine pearls,
emeralds or sapphires, wretchedly set and often pierced
through the middle or strung on pack thread; but still
genuine precious stones. No Arab will wear a *false*
stone, and for that reason they prefer that they should
not match, as they always suspect the regularity of our
English jewels. As to their position with regard to
the other sex, it is no better than that of the Arabs.

They are utterly uneducated, and the rich and those of
high rank never leave their own houses. We went to
see one of them, the Princess . . . . . who had a little
girl of five, who was *fiancée* to a little boy-cousin of six,
the most sulky impersonation I ever saw of a small
Moor. This lady told us that formerly she had been
allowed by her husband to go on the terrace of her
house, but that now it had been glazed over. She had
never seen any of her own relations since she was a
little child, and never went beyond those four walls.
If the parents are poor, the advent of a girl is looked
upon as a positive misfortune by both Arabs and
Moors. When a boy comes into the world, the wife is
presented with a beautiful circular brooch to fasten her
haïk; but blows and a curse are her only reward for
producing one of the other sex. Madame Luce and
the Sisters of Charity are striving to raise these poor
little things from this miserable position, and by teaching them needlework and embroidery to enable them
to get situations in better-class houses. One of these
children was a servant in the Princess' household
which I have just mentioned, and a more faultlessly
beautiful face I never saw, with soft almond-shaped
eyes and the most winning smile. But alas! for her,
poor child, should her master cast his eyes upon her
beauty!

Another remarkable race in Algiers are the Jews. I

have already described the dress of the women in my
account of the marriage. The men are the same all
over the world ; hook-nosed, dark-eyed, and sallow ;
they swarm in the bazaars and hold most of the principal stalls. Under the Mussulman rule, they suffered
every kind of indignity and persecution ; but with that
wonderful patience and tenacity which characterise
their race, they lived on and became useful and even
necessary to their persecutors through their intimate
knowledge of all commercial concerns, which fell almost
entirely into their hands. The French, by striving to
conciliate them and raise their position, have offended
the strongest Mussulman prejudices ; and it is doubtful
whether they can ever be safely admitted in this country to share in European privileges.

But I am forgetting the most important of the
Algerian races ; the Berbers or Kabyles. I shall
devote a separate chapter to them and to their country.
But in Algiers, they are distinguished by their striped
black and white woollen haïks and burnous, their
leather aprons, and their bare and often shaved heads.
They are far more industrious than the Arabs, and are
employed in every kind of trade ; but I cannot say that
they are either as handsome or as picturesque in appearance. Their wives walk about with their faces uncovered, but we saw very few of them in Algiers
itself.

The number of negroes has diminished in the town in proportion to the smaller number of caravans which arrive from the interior; but there are still a good number employed in the Turkish baths and as domestic servants, as well as in certain trades—such as white-washing, &c. Negresses are invariably employed as sellers of bread: squatted outside the town, covered from head to foot in their blue-checked burnouses striped with red, their broad laughing faces and thick lips may be seen at any hour of the day with great baskets of flat circular loaves by their side, screaming, gesticulating, and selling, all at the same time. I have already mentioned them in the baths and in their seashore sacrifices. They always realised one's idea of the witches of one's youthful imagination; but I believe that, as domestic servants, they are both faithful and devoted.

But we have not half done with the motley tribes which shoulder one another as we toil up the steep Arab streets or wander through the ever-amusing bazaars. There are the Biskris, like the 'hamals' or porters of Constantinople, struggling under weights, which to ordinary mortals would be impossible; the water-carriers or Zibanis, with their picturesque brass water-jars poised on their shoulders; the Mzabi, with their files of donkeys, or sitting behind their stalls, gaily piled with oranges, water melons, and fan palm-leaves ; or else by their smoking cook-shops, in which infinitesimal little bits of meat are for ever frizzling on tiny skewers, set upright, all of a row, for the delectation of the passers-by; the Lar'ouatis, or dealers in oil, the traces of whose occupation may generally be seen on their clothes ; the Mzitis, with their great sacks of wheat, by the side of which their patient camels may be seen wearily resting, and occasionally growling and showing their teeth as one brushes by them : all these many and divers tribes, each with his distinctive dress and habits, though classified by the guide-books under the generic name of Berranis, form the most animated and beautiful groups at all times of the day in Algiers, but especially in the early morning, when buyers and sellers are in full activity ; or later by the fountains, where each and all come to rest and refresh themselves, when the noon-day sun has driven most of the Europeans to seek the shelter of their houses.

As to society in Algiers, we were not fair judges ; for in the first place we went for health and wished to remain quiet ; and in the second, it was, as I have before said, a time of war and revolution. Ordinarily, I believe, nothing can be more agreeable than the military society of the place, and the kindness of Maréchal MacMahon (the late governor) and that of his wife had been extended to every one who had sought for change and warmth by passing 'a winter

among the swallows.' But some of the old *régime*
were still left, with whom we made acquaintance : the
gallant old Admiral of the Port, Fabre la Maurelle,
with his two charming daughters, who occupy the
Admiralty House on the port, with its green latticed
harem windows, and ancient chapel, which served
formerly as a prison to the Christian slaves and con-
fessors for the faith under the Mussulman rule ; the
Lord Chief Justice, M. Pierrey, who combines the
most varied and extensive information with an intimate
acquaintance with all the most eminent men of the
day, and lives with his excellent and devoted wife in
the most beautiful Moorish house in Algiers, the perfection of which their own good taste has known how
to enhance in a thousand ways ; and Madame Yussuf,
widow of the famous general of that name, who still
inhabits the lovely Moorish country house at Mustapha
Supérieur, of which her husband had been so proud,
and which he had fitted up with the beautiful *thuya*
wood (a species of dark-grained cedar), of which we
had seen so much on our way to Teniet-el-Hâd. But
now her home is for ever desolate, and, in the exquisite
chapel she has built to his memory in the garden, and
in continual works of piety and charity, she finds her
only real consolation. We went one day to the country
palace of the governor at Mustapha Supérieur, to
return the civility of its new occupier who had

been our travelling companion from Oran ; and his
wife good-naturedly took us over the whole building, which was formerly the magnificent palace of the
Deys, and is one of the finest specimens of a Moorish
house possible ; with beautiful hanging gardens which
are open to the public on certain days, and a whole
avenue of camellias in the fullest blossom.   The lovely
' bourgainvillier' with its bright lilac leaves, covered
the walls of this wonderful garden, which boasts of
some of the finest palms in Algiers.   A little lower
down is the quaint Moorish house where poor Made-
moiselle Tinié lived for a year as an Arab lady,
surrounded by retainers of the same nation, before she
started on that unhappy expedition on the frontiers of
Tripoli which ended in her murder.   She was too
ready to trust every one who came near her ; and,
though warned by the English consul of the probable
consequences of carrying so much treasure along with
her among those half-civilised tribes, would not hearken
to his warnings and paid for her temerity with her life.
The Vice-Consul, Mr. Elmore, has a pretty Moorish
house on the other side of the road, which he has fitted
up with every English comfort, and which is well adap-
ted to English habits.   This house is now to let, and
would be invaluable to invalids proceeding to pass the
winter in Algiers.   For however fascinating these
Moorish houses may be, seen in a hot summer's day, or

towards the end of spring, it must be remembered that
in winter they are generally intensely cold ; that there
is no means of warming them ; and that though the
weather is, generally speaking, delicious in this country,
there are days and even weeks of wet and cold, when
a fire is not only a luxury, but a positive necessity.
The only two regular Moorish country houses I saw
which had that luxury, were Lady L. T——'s, and
Mr. Elmore's. The latter has turned the usual upper
court into a drawing-room and roofed it ; while he has
built out a dining-room with a pretty passage leading
to it, in which he has introduced the picturesque Moorish arches, the whole thing being done in perfect taste,
and yet combined with very comfortable English fire-
places ! I am afraid my readers will think this a very
prosaic view to take of what is certainly most tempting
in the neighbourhood of Algiers. But I write it for
the sake of the many invalids, who, since my return,
have questioned me as to the advisability or not of
taking houses there for the winter. And to them all I
say deliberately, ' do not dream of taking a pretty
Moorish house, unless there be some means of warming it.' The wisest plan would be to take apartments
in the Hôtel d'Orient, where they will find every
luxury, moderate charges, and an excellent *table
d'hôte*, until they can look about them and choose for
themselves.

CHAPTER IV.

THE CHARITABLE INSTITUTIONS OF ALGIERS.

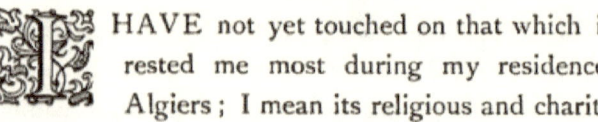 HAVE not yet touched on that which inte-
rested me most during my residence in
Algiers; I mean its religious and charitable
institutions. But I will devote a separate chapter to
the subject, which those who are not interested in it
can simply skip; while those who are, may care to
have some details as to the great works which are
being carried on for God in this, the former stronghold
of Mahometan infidelity.

I have already spoken of the famine which decimated
Algeria three or four years ago, and in which such
thousands of Arabs perished. People attributed it in
part to the three years of drought which had succeeded
each other; and in part to the way in which the Arabs
had been tempted by the high prices of corn to sell
their usual hoards in the French markets. But from
whatever cause this terrible calamity arose, its results
were the same. The French clergy and sisters, with

MOORISH INTERIOR.

the Archbishop at their head, multiplied themselves to meet the distress ; pitched tents everywhere for the distribution of provisions and clothes ; and, by incredible toil and self-denial, saved the lives of many.

But thousands died in spite of all their efforts ; and their poor little skin-and-bone children, looking more like starved monkeys than human beings, were left, fatherless and motherless, without food, clothes, or shelter, to the charity of the Christians. We know that this charity has never yet failed, and we all recollect the superhuman exertions made by the Archbishop and others, not only in Algeria, but throughout Europe, to collect funds to provide for this multitude of little ones so suddenly thrown on their hands. But this Archbishop is not only a devoted priest and father of his flock ; he is also a great administrator. He looked round his diocese and saw how much might be done by the cultivation of even a small portion of the enormous quantity of waste land lying fallow almost up to the very gates of Algiers ; and he resolved to purchase large tracts of country and to place his orphanages in the centre of each ; so that, as the children grew older and stronger, they might clear and till the ground around them, and so by degrees make their homes self-supporting. The plan he had thus conceived and matured, he lost no time in putting into execution ; and God has crowned his labours with such unparalleled success, that it is almost impossible to believe that so short a time has elapsed since their commencement.

The first of these orphanages which I was taken to see was that of St. Charles, in the hills beyond Birmandraïs, about seven or eight miles from Algiers. Mdlle. de St. Paulet (the daughter of the Marquis de St. Paulet) had begged in England for this home, which consists of 300 or 400 Arab girls, who are employed mainly in agricultural work under the care of the sisters of St. Charles. They have two or three hours' schooling in the day and receive a simple and useful education in reading, writing, and needlework, besides, of course, religious instruction. But the greater portion of their time is spent in the cultivation of the vineyards and garden, in the care of the dairy, and in all kinds of farm work. In this they are instructed by a new religious Order, instituted by the Archbishop for both men and women, called after the martyr of Algiers, *Geronimo*; the Brothers and Sisters of this Order wear the Arab dress and devote themselves entirely to the education of children in every species of industrial and out-of-door work.

Mdlle. Anna Fabre la Maurelle, the daughter of the Admiral of the Port and a most holy and devoted person, is one of the main supporters of this orphanage, the poverty of which is extreme—but the children all

looked well and healthy. On my objecting to so much
out-of-door work for girls, I was told that only those
were sent to St. Charles whose state of health and
vitiated blood rendered out-of-door employment absolutely necessary to their well-being.

On our return, we stopped to see what I may call
the Sister Establishment to that of St. Charles—that is,
the enormous orphanage of Ma Sœur Chavanne, of the
Order of St. Vincent of Paul (the friend and companion at the seminary in Paris of the present Superior of
the orphanage in Carlisle Place), who received 500 or
600 of the Archbishop's little Arabs in a beautiful old
Moorish house assigned to them by General MacMahon
at Mustapha Supérieur. There the children are
taught every kind of home employment, and their
needlework is quite beautiful. But lest they should
suffer from too much confinement, they have a very
large garden, a dairy, and poultry yard; all of which is
cultivated and cared for by the girls themselves.
There are ten or twelve Sisters of Charity in this
house, which is managed with that perfection which all
who know the works of those sisters will understand.
Before I leave the subject of Monseigneur's Arab girls,
I will mention one more home for them in Algiers
itself, near the Kasba, which was founded by Mdme. la
Maréchale MacMahon (as the Duchess of Magenta is
always called here), who placed them also under the

care of the Sisters of Charity, and mainly contributed
to their support.   The Superior, Ma Sœur Pauline, is
a most charming and remarkable person, speaking
Arabic as well as her own language ; and so immensely
beloved by the Arabs (whom she visits in their
homes in sickness and in health), that they would do
anything to oblige or help her.   There is a day school
attached to this orphanage ; but the Sisters have the
mortification of being prohibited from giving the
children any religious instruction, and are forced to
limit their charitable efforts to making them *morally*
good as far as they can, and saving them from the fate
which often awaits these poor girls in their Mahometan
homes.   The Sisters enforce respectable marriages and
endeavour to defer them till they are fourteen or
fifteen ; so that much good is actually done ; although
in a manner so uncongenial to their own feelings.

I must now go back to the other and more important
half of the Archbishop's labours, and that is, the care
and education of the Arab boys.   For this purpose he
bought 1,300 acres of land near the ' Maison Carrée,'
which is the first station on the railroad from Algiers
to Blidah.   Here he established first 700 and then
1,000 of these little orphans, placing them under the
care of these same fathers and brothers of ' Geronimo;'
and the results are perfectly incredible.   In spite of
the sandy and arid nature of a large portion of the

ground which is near the sea, and of the apparently
hopeless task of clearing the dense masses of fan palm
and squill (which, as I have before said, form the
'bush' or 'scrub' of Algeria, the root of the latter
being as big as a child's head), they have succeeded in
reclaiming and cultivating almost the whole of this
immense tract of country and making it look like a
beautiful market garden. When I first drove to the
farm, I found acres upon acres of green peas, beans,
and artichokes, which a certain number of the boys
were gathering for the French market, under the superintendence of a father wearing the usual white Arab
dress; while another set were digging a big field
beyond and preparing it for future crops. They have
250 acres of beautiful wheat, which was then in full
ear; a large dairy; eleven mules and thirty-five oxen;
an extensive vineyard producing excellent wine; and
workshops where the boys are taught every description
of trade—carpentering, masonry, tailoring, shoe-making;
&c., &c. They have a blacksmith's forge; and make
everything they use or wear; and produce everything
they eat. They have also a fine flock of sheep and
goats. Their last and most important work has been
building their own college, and that of the fathers,
which they have very nearly completed; as well as a
small house for the Archbishop, who, though absent at
the time I was there, was kept most minutely informed of

everything that went on and was the life and soul, as he had been the creator, of the establishment. To prove the healthiness of the children, the Superior took me into the infirmary where, out' of all this large number of boys, there were only two or three beds occupied, and those with patients suffering from slight disease.

There are eleven fathers and six lay-brothers to superintend this great orphanage, which is now entirely self-supporting and will soon bring in a good profit. But the Archbishop has not contented himself with housing and feeding this, his numerous family; he has likewise made provision for their future needs. It was objected to him that the Arab girls brought up and educated as Christians would have no chance of settling in life; the Arabs as Mahometans would scorn them; and the Europeans would object to choosing wives, almost the whole of whom are tattooed on the face with the distinctive marks of their tribe. To meet this difficulty, the Archbishop has bought a large tract of land in the neighbourhood of Miliana, divided it off in plots and means eventually to build little houses on each. Then when his orphans are of a marriageable age, he means to marry his boys to his girls, give them each, as a *dot*, one of these little properties (which both will have learnt to cultivate), and thus eventually form an Arab Christian population in the very heart of Algeria. I can only hope that this, the crowning point of his philanthropic plan, may be as successful as all the preliminary stages have been.

I had a long conversation with the Superior of the Boys' Orphanage, who kindly took me over the Establishment ; and he told me that their only difficulty that year would be how to get in their wheat crop, which was so heavy, as they had no machine for reaping. And this is on a soil where, four years ago, nothing grew but palms and weeds !

I have already mentioned the Archbishop's seminary at Koubba, where thirty or forty of the most intelligent of these Arab boys are preparing for the priesthood, who will hereafter be valuable auxiliaries to the missions among the natives. There is another large seminary adjoining the Archbishop's country house on the opposite side of Algiers, above the Faubourg St. Eugène. It is on a rising ground overlooking the sea, with a large and extensive garden and a glorious view ; but both the Archbishop and the students were away when I visited it, although his good old house-keeper allowed me to see the interior of the building, where I found a fine full length portrait of the Martyr Geronimo. This seminary is close to ' Notre Dame d'Afrique,' a magnificent church on the hill above Algiers, built with Cupolas in the Moorish style, and served by Religious. There is a little chapel alongside, where there is a miraculous image of Our Lady, which is a favourite place of pilgrimage and is covered with 'ex-votos.' The Archbishop has founded a mass in perpetuity every Saturday in this church for the souls of those who have died at sea, the names of each being inscribed in a register kept for that purpose.

A little lower down the hill is another Arab Orphanage for girls, kept by some ladies who devote themselves to this work in the same way as Mdlle. de Tuliére at Vicarage Place, Kensington, without wearing a distinctive religious dress. They have a work-room likewise in the town, where the children are taught dress-making and millinery ; in which they have been eminently successful.

The Archbishop's beautiful palace in Algiers had been turned into an ambulance for the sick and wounded while I was there; and the Moorish Quadrangle and Galleries were crammed with boys taught by the Christian brothers, who had been turned out of their regular class rooms by the so-called Liberal Government. I could not help feeling how characteristic the house was of a true Pastor of a flock, sheltering, as it did, the suffering and the little ones under his own roof.

So much for the instruction and care of the Arab orphans. But how shall I describe the other schools and charitable institutions of Algiers without wearying

my readers ?   The Sisters of Charity of St. Vincent of
Paul, under Ma Sœur Barbe, the Provincial, have thousands of children under instruction ; besides a
Foundling Hospital, a Dispensary, a Crèche, the Civil
and Military Hospitals, and all those beautiful works
of Christian love to which they devote their whole
lives, whether in London's murky courts or under an
African sun.   But when I was there, they were in
great trouble.   The Revolutionary Government had
closed their schools and made them give up their
beautiful large class rooms to secular teachers.   But
the children followed the Sisters, in spite of the Government ; and through the indefatigable exertions of the
holy Curé of the Cathedral, M. de Matignon, one or
two small Moorish houses were obtained in different
parts of the town, to which the Sisters daily repaired
and where the children were huddled, upstairs and
down, in the courts, on the roofs, and, in fact, wherever
there was standing room.   I thought with terror of
what would happen to both Sisters and children when
the hot season began.   But I hope by that time a
change of Government will have restored to them their
airy school rooms.   The last act of oppression of which
the authorities were guilty whilst I was there, was the
closing of the Sisters' Dispensary, which was attended
daily by hundreds of poor of every nation.   At the
Council, when this proposal came under discussion, the

so-called Christians, to their shame be it spoken, all voted for the suppression of the Charity, and only the Mahometans spoke in favour of it! One of the Council declared that the *moral* effect of the Sisters upon the people was bad. Boukadoura, one of the principal Arab gentlemen of Algiers, wittily replied: 'Mais, Monsieur, elles ne se mêlent que de la Physique!'

As usual, the Sisters only repay the ill-usage they receive by increased kindness. At Mustapha Inférieur, where Ma Sœur Felicité is the Superior, and where they have another immense establishment, they had been equally turned out of their class rooms, when one of the most violent of their opponents was thrown from his horse just opposite their door, and so tenderly nursed and cared for by them, that he lost no time on his recovery in reinstating them in their schools; but this was a solitary exception. I could not help being struck by a remark made to me one day by an Arab gentleman who was speaking indignantly of the treatment of the Clergy and Sisters by the authorities:

'I don't understand you Christians,' he exclaimed. 'We have plenty of strife and dissensions among ourselves, certainly; but we consider that religion is in a region apart from and above all that; a thing, in fact, too sacred to be meddled with. Whereas you, *vous en voulez toujours en* **premier à votre religion !** ' (the first thing you attack is your religion).

I might have replied that it was an evidence of the truth of our faith that the enemy of all good was ever stirring up the bitterest animosity against it in the minds of men, but refrained. It is curious how identical the persecution of the Church is in every land, and how under pretence of ' Liberty,' the most oppressive enactments are always being carried out against every kind of religion ; but to return to our Sisters of Charity. Their military hospital is one of the most magnificent establishments possible, being situated in the palace and gardens formerly occupied by the Dey of Algiers and his harem. The wards are very large and airy, and beautifully kept, with spacious corridors for the patients to smoke and walk in hot weather ; and the pleasure grounds are equally enjoyable. There were a very large number of French wounded when we were there and still more of small-pox patients, who were arriving daily in ship-loads from the seat of war ; and one felt what a blessed change for them this beautiful hospital must be, in such a delicious climate, after the sufferings they had endured from cold and wet on the battle field ! The only thing which is badly arranged is the chapel, which is poor and ugly ; and the Sisters' quarters are not as healthy as they should be, being built only one story high with the drainage of the hill just above them; the consequence is, that the Superior, who is not strong, is always suffering from fever. The officers' wards are in a separate and very beautiful Moorish building, which was formerly the Dey's own apartment; with a lovely court shaded by palms and orange-trees and covered with beautiful creepers.

Besides the numerous establishments of the Sisters of Charity, there are the large schools of the Sisters of the 'Doctrine Chrétienne,' whose 'Mother-House' is in Mustapha Supérieur, where they have a most glorious garden and view. Then there are the Sisters of the 'Good Shepherd,' who are at El Biar, a village to the north of Algiers; the 'Little Sisters of the Poor,' who have a fine Moorish house with a glorious view between Algiers and Bou Zarea, with 200 or 300 old people of both sexes; the 'Dames du Sacré Cœur,' who have a large 'Pensionnat' for young ladies at the foot of Mustapha Supérieur; and last not least 'Les Sœurs du Bon Secours,' who live in a delicious Moorish house in the town at the back of the new University. Their Superior had just returned from the French 'Ambulance,' where she had nursed, among others, General Mac Mahon himself, and had very narrowly escaped being shot by the Prussians, of which she gave us an amusing account. She was returning to Metz when they missed a French officer, a prisoner on parole, and insisted upon it that the poor sister was this

very individual in disguise. In vain she protested.
She was condemned to be shot at six o'clock the
following morning. At last, a young officer took pity
upon her and asked her if there were no one in the
town who could vouch for her identity? She fortunately remembered a friend there, whose address she
gave; and was at once conducted to this lady's house
with a file of twenty men, ten on each side of the
carriage door. ' On ne m'a jamais fait tant d'honneur!'
she said laughing. Fortunately her friend was at home,
and the instant recognition produced an order for her
release, and an apology from the Germans: so that
she was ' quitte pour la peur.'

Before concluding this chapter, I must mention one
more religious foundation which has contributed perhaps
as much as any other to the welfare of Algiers. I mean
the Trappist monastery of Staouëli. In that pleasant
little book of Miss Edwards, ' A Winter Among the
Swallows,' a separate chapter is devoted to her visit
there, and I can scarcely wonder at the admiration and
interest it excited, even in the mind of a Protestant.

Leaving Algiers by the street called Bab-el-Oued,
and passing by the great military hospital which I have
before described, we came to the first Christian cemetery,
to which an interesting story is attached. The ground,
which is enclosed by an aloe-hedge, was purchased in
the sixteenth century by a devoted Capuchin father

(the confessor of Duke John of Austria), with the price
of his ransom; he having freely elected to remain
and suffer all the ill-usage and indignities of a slave, so
that his fellow-prisoners should have the consolation of
decent Christian burial in consecrated ground, instead
of their bodies being thrown, as heretofore, into the
sea.   Above, towers the Church of Notre Dame
d'Afrique, and the country house and seminary of the
Archbishop.   But the road we were following passes
through the pretty Faubourg of St. Eugène, with its
villas enclosed in luxuriant gardens and orange-groves,
till it reaches the *Point Pescade*, where a beautiful old
Moorish fort juts out into the sea. We had breakfasted
at a picturesque *café* here a few days before, as it is a
favourite drive from Algiers.   So far, all was lovely.
The little bays, their sandy shores covered with cowries
and other shells, were sparkling like turquoises in the
bright sun.   Multitudes of fishing boats with their
picturesque lateen sails were reflected in the still blue
water, while a variety of sea birds were skimming over
the surface, apparently sharing in the hauls of the
fishermen.   It was like a little bit of the Corniche
road; the shore being studded with picturesque
Moorish houses, with here and there tempting-looking
wooded dells and streams and narrow valleys leading
up to the hills above.   But after leaving the Point, the
country became at once deserted, desolate, and utterly

uncultivated. The fan palm resumed its reign of
' bush ' and ' scrub,' and for miles of monotonous road
nothing else was to be seen, till we suddenly turned
to the left and came upon a great wooden cross, when
the whole character of the place seemed changed.
Acres of magnificent crops, beautiful vineyards, shady
fig-trees, great fields of sweet-scented geranium (planted
in ridge and furrow, like beans, and cultivated for
making essence), lined the road on both sides. A little
further on large flocks of cattle and pigs were feeding,
tended by their silent herdsmen ; and soon we came to
a great walled enclosure of fifty acres, containing the
monastery, cemetery, orangery, and private gardens of
the Trappists, into which no woman may enter but by
papal permission. The magnificent palms in the
courtyard and the beautiful cypress avenue leading to
their cemetery were visible from the outside of the
enclosure.

When in 1830 the French accomplished their landing
at the Cape of Sidi Ferruch, the Moslem army was
camped at Staouëli, and a battle was fought on this
spot which ended in the success of the French and
decided the fate of Algiers. Thirteen years later about
a thousand acres of this apparently hopeless desert
land was conceded to the Trappists ; and on August 19,
1843, the little colony arrived, under the care of
their holy Superior, the Reverend Francis Regis, and

pitching a tent in the midst of the waste, offered the
first Holy Sacrifice for the repose of the souls of those
who had there fallen in battle.   Nothing could be more
disheartening, apparently, than the appearance of the
new colony, or more arduous than the task they had
proposed to themselves of clearing this tangled ground
and preparing it for any sort of cultivation.   But what
will not charity and holy toil accomplish ?   The
Superior was a man in all ways equal to the undertaking, and in three years this desert had been converted as if by magic into the magnificent property
which we now saw.   The first stone of the abbey was
laid on a bed of shells and balls found on the battle-
field.   It is a rectangular building of fifty square yards,
the centre being occupied by a garden surrounded by
an open cloister with double arches, the work of an
Italian father who died in 1848.   One wing is devoted
to the chapel ; the rest to the refectory, kitchen, and
cells of the monks, which are of the most primitive and
simple kind.   On the wall of the refectory are inscribed
the words, 'If it be sad to live at La Trappe, it is
sweet to die here.'   To the left of the abbey are large
farm buildings, granaries, and stalls for cattle ; beyond
are the orchards and vineyards, the latter producing
annually an immense quantity of the best wine, which
forms the principal revenue of the monastery.   They
employ and relieve all the Arabs who come to their

gate, and have in reality changed the whole face of the country; only proving what may be done in this glorious soil and climate with a little energy, perseverance, and labour. The present Superior, a very gentlemanlike, intelligent man, received us at the arched gateway and conducted us to a little outside building intended for visitors, courteously expressing his regret at his inability to receive ladies inside the enclosure, but desiring the porter to open the principal gates that we might see the beautiful palm tree in the courtyard (supposed to be the largest in Algiers) which shades a graceful statue of our Lady called ' Notre Dame de Staouëli.' He gave us an interesting account of their work which every day increases in magnitude. They have now 110 choir fathers, besides lay brothers; and employ upwards of 170 poor Arabs, French, and Spaniards as labourers; some of whom are Arab prisoners sent by the Government to work out their sentence after a certain time of proved good conduct. We had brought our luncheon with us, to the distress of the Superior, who was hospitably having some fish, omelettes, and cheese prepared for us. I was amused at the dismay of our courier when he was preparing to unpack a chicken he had brought for us and was stopped by the brother porter, with the oracular words, ' *Les poulets n'entrent pas !* ' As it was Shrove Tuesday we thought it rather hard, but the Superior explained

that the *maigre* of the house was never allowed to be
infringed all the year round ; and that if strangers were
to leave behind any portion of the meat in their baskets
abuses might creep in.   He made amends by bringing
us excellent bread and butter, coffee, and oranges,
together with some of the most delicious wine, from
their own vintage, I ever drank.   They have a touching custom at Staouëli when men come to stay with
them as visitors, whether poor or rich, to prostrate
themselves flat on the ground before their guests, thus
recognising in them the person of Our Blessed Lord.
The Superior told me that they had a very large number
of Postulants every year, some of whom remained,
but others did not; that several among them were
Zouaves, and that they made it a rule to refuse no one
who asked for admittance, leaving it to time to ascertain their inclination or fitness for the Order.   The
rule of silence is absolute within the enclosure except
to the Superior ; and the daily duties of each of the
brothers are written down and hung in the cloister to
which each repairs after mass and office.   In spite of
the hardships of their life they seem in general healthy
and well.   The old and infirm amongst them are
employed in carving and making rosaries of cowrie
shells, which they sell for the benefit of the poor who
throng their gates.   It is curious that the only serious
attempt at cultivation in the neighbourhood of Algiers

should have been undertaken by monks and priests! But so it is, and they have amply proved, both at Staouéli and the Maison Carrée, what may be done with this soil, if only sufficient labour and care be bestowed upon it.

The whole subject of French colonisation in Algeria seems to have been misunderstood; but while it is not difficult to find fault with the present uncultivated state of three-fourths of this beautiful country, it is not so easy to find a remedy. Some people attribute it entirely to the military government of the country. But we must recollect first, that Algeria had to be conquered, step by step, from the Arabs: next, that a *civil* authority is rarely respected by those warlike tribes, whose sole idea of power consists in a greater or lesser number of guns. 'They laugh at a Frenchman in a frock-coat,' said one very intelligent man to me, with whom I had a long talk on this subject, 'but a uniform at once ensures their respect.' On the other hand, it has been a great mistake to send from France as colonists, men without capital, and often broken down in character, health, and fortunes. Algeria has been looked upon by the Imperial Government, less as a colony than as a place for *déportés* and political offenders, whose misdemeanours were not sufficiently grave to entitle them to banishment to Cayenne, but who still were dangerous to the peace of France. Hence the

I 2

strong revolutionary and communistic element now
existing in that country and hence also, the multitudes of 'Cafés' and 'Billiards' which meet one at
every turn, often half in ruins ; but the keeping of
which seems to be the only employment for which such
a class of persons is fitted. But even respectable
colonists or emigrants have great difficulties to contend
with, though they are stated differently by different
people. One man attributed his failure to the cum-
brous duties and prohibitions of the French Custom-
House, and the heavy differential port dues levied on
all foreign shipping. 'French colonists,' he remarked,
' pay enormously for everything they consume or use,
if not produced in Algeria ; while they have to sell at
a much less profit when they export, on account of the
absurdly heavy port dues and freight and commission
expenses. Hundreds of foreign vessels,' he added,
' now pass by the Algerian ports who would gladly
enter and trade and take in cargo, were it not for the
port dues.' On the other hand a very intelligent and
clever English gentleman, a Mr. M——, who has
taken a large farm in the neighbourhood of Kolea,
thinks that the fault lies with the French colonists
themselves, and declares that the protective duties are
next to nothing for steam machinery or tools, of which
he has imported large quantities from England. He
says that when a Frenchman buys or gets a grant of

land, he never lives there himself, but sublets it to another man, who again under-lets it to a third : so that the original proprietor has no interest in the place whatever, and three profits must be extracted from the land instead of one. His own difficulty lies in want of labourers. He began by importing Englishmen with their families and settling them most comfortably on his new farm. But this farm is in the Plain of the Mitidja, which at certain seasons of the year is very unhealthy. The first man caught the fever and died ; the rest took a panic and lost heart, and finally the whole set insisted on returning home. Then he tried Arabs, but, though they were willing to herd cattle, they would not work. He has now got Frenchmen at 1*l*. a week, and Spaniards for hedging and ditching. But he has great difficulty in getting foreigners to understand the machinery he brought from England, and which yet would be so invaluable in a country where hands are so scarce.[1]

While I was in Algiers, I was asked if I would undertake to send a certain number of our overplus population as emigrants to this country. But I found that though the Committee were anxious enough for English labourers, they had no sort of organisation to receive them on their arrival. And to turn an English

---

[1] Since this was written, I hear that Mr. M—— has given up his farm to his French partner.

workman out of a ship on a strange shore, of which he
knows neither the people nor the language, without
anyone to guide or direct him, would be simply
absurd. La Maréchale MacMahon did this with some
Irishmen a few years ago, and the poor fellows were
sent to an unhealthy district, caught the fever, and
those who did not die were speedily invalided home
again. It seems a thousand pities, certainly, that such
a glorious country should be allowed to lie waste for
want of hands, when you have only, as they say, to
'scratch' the ground to produce the most beautiful
crops imaginable, while hundreds of our fellow-country-
men are starving at home for want of work. But,
unless there be some arrangement made to receive,
protect, and look after the interests of the English
emigrants on their arrival, the experiment must inevit-
ably end in failure and cruel disappointment.

I have not alluded to one cause of the failure of the
French colonists, but which yet is a more serious one
than all the rest, and that is the incendiary fires.
Often, when the crops are just ready for the sickle, the
Arabs will come secretly and set fire to the whole field,
destroying all the hopes of the farmer in one night.
We saw whole blackened tracts of wood near Marengo
utterly ruined in this way, which is certainly disheartening enough to deter the most enterprising colonist.

We must hope, however, that the result of the late

insurrection will be the settlement of affairs on a surer
footing; and that the late importation of Alsatians (which
was beginning when I left) may by their persevering
industry change by degrees the aspect of the country.
Algeria can hardly yet be said to be settled, or to have
emerged from the state of a country which has been
conquered by force of arms; and till peace is fairly
established little or nothing can be done for its colonisation.

KABYLE POTS.

CHAPTER V.

CHERCHEL AND TIZI-OZOUN.

TWO of the most charming expeditions to be made from Algiers, though in exactly opposite directions, are to the Roman antiquities of Cherchel on one side, and to the picturesque Kabylia mountains on the other. Each takes four or five days to do comfortably, and there is no difficulty in hiring a little carriage in Algiers for this purpose, and by making arrangements with the authorities to obtain a relay of horses on the road. Our first expedition was to Cherchel and the 'Tomb of the Christian,' which we had seen so often on the horizon and with which we were longing to make a nearer acquaintance.

Taking the upper road to Staouëli and passing by the villages of El Biar and Cheraga, we soon left the fertile farm and vineyards of the Trappists, and emerged into the open country which was desolate and uncultivated as usual, till we had passed a picturesque bridge over a river called L'Oued-Mazafran; after which the fan palms were exchanged for large fields of wheat, tobacco, and cotton. Arrived at Kolea, where we were to sleep, we found a pretty little town perched on one of the hills of the Sahel range, looking over the great Mitidja plain towards Blidah, with a tidy little mosque and Moorish fountain, a koubba shaded by palms, and a cypress tree of which the seed is said to have been brought from Mecca. After walking through the town and engaging the only two available rooms in the very humble inn, we took fresh horses and drove on to the 'Tomb of the Christian,' which is about eighteen miles from Kolea. The road passes through miles of lentisk and dwarf palms, only enlivened here and there by Arab 'gourbis,' crammed full of natives watching their flocks, or drinking coffee squatted in solemn rows, their brown faces alone peering out of the voluminous folds of their burnouses. The road was so utterly desolate and deserted, that I was not without some sort of anxiety as to the intentions of our dusky friends, and subsequent events proved that my apprehensions were not unfounded. It was a relief to come at last to the large farm buildings of the English gentleman of whom I have before spoken, and who had lately gone into partnership with a French colonist; although the high looped walls round the enclosure spoke of the need of defence in case of incendiary fires or attacks of the tribes. To the left, was the large and

stagnant lake of Halloula, famous for its wild ducks
and its leeches ; but still more for the fevers which,
in summer, are exhaled from its fetid waters. On
nearing the tomb, we were told that the late heavy
rains had washed away the regular road, but that there
was a short cut up the hills through the thick brush-
wood, known to the Arabs, which would lead us to the
spot. Stopping at a ' Café Maure ' by the side of the
road, we accordingly hired a guide, who led us by a
tremendously steep path under a burning sun to the
top. The appearance of this mausoleum from a
distance is that of a gigantic circular haystack. On
drawing near we found that it was composed of a series
of steps, fifty-three in number (each step as deep as
those of the Egyptian pyramids), placed in a circle of
sixty yards round the summit which appeared like an
immense depressed cone. It had originally twelve
sides. The principal entrance is by a low, heavy,
massive door, with large circular pillars on either side,
forming probably part of an ancient portico. By
creeping in almost on hands and knees you come into
a large circular chamber with smaller ones opening out
of it, evidently intended as vaults for the reception of
human bodies. After a great deal of controversy on
the subject it has, I believe, been now proved beyond
doubt that this curious mausoleum was built by Juba II.
King of Mauritania, about the year 26 B.C. as a burial-

place for himself and his family; the absurd name given to it being a corruption of ' Kbour-er-Roumia,' or ' Kbour-Roumim,' meaning ' The tomb of Kings and of the mighty upon Earth.' Of course there are endless Arab legends attached to it, and a firm belief in their minds that untold treasures in gold and silver are concealed therein. These stories came to the ears of a Pacha in the sixteenth century, who sent a number of workmen to effect an opening into the mausoleum and bring forth the concealed treasure. But scarcely had the men begun their work when they were struck with terror by a spectral figure appearing on the summit of the tomb, which, stretching its arms towards the lake, exclaimed, ' Halloula! Halloula! Help!' The answer was a swarm of mosquitoes darkening the whole air, of so deadly and ferocious a kind that the affrighted workmen fled from the spot and could not be persuaded to return.

We listened to this legend as we sat on one of the gigantic pillars lying about the ruins and looked down on the grand view below. To the north was the bright blue Mediterranean and the rocks of Cherchel jutting out into the sea; to the south was the magnificent plain of the Mitidja bounded by the great chain of the Atlas Mountains; while a soft haze from the lake below rose over the woods which fringed its borders and gave to the whole that misty middle-

distance-look, which is generally wanting in African
landscapes.   The view was certainly worth the toil of
the weary climb to the top, but we were desperately
tired by the time we reached Kolea that evening, and
not inclined to find fault with the primitive accommodation of the little inn.   One thing in Algeria is much
to be commended; the beds are invariably clean and
good, and you find no occupants in them but your-
selves.   We wish as much could be said by travellers
in Italy and Spain.

The next morning I went early to the pretty little
church near the Botanical Garden, and there found
again the sisters of the ' Doctrine Chrétienne,' who
have a nice school close to the church.   At seven
o'clock we started for Cherchel, stopping to bait our
horses and eat our luncheon at Marengo, a pretty little
village situated at the extreme western end of the
Plain of the Mitidja and at the foot of the beautiful
mountains of Beni-Menacer.   Here we found a large
establishment of the sisters of charity of St. Vincent
of Paul, who have a charming Superior (Ma Sœur
Courtés) and nine sisters, in charge of the great civil
hospital, (which then contained about ninety fever
patients, besides accidents, &c.,) an orphanage, a
' Maternité,' an Arab hospital, and large national
and infant schools.   They have a beautiful dairy-farm,
and garden, and were most kind to us; giving us

breakfast, and loading us with fresh flowers and delicious butter of their own making—a rare luxury in that country! They told us that the neighbouring woods and plains were rife with fever, and that even then their hospital was full, although it was much worse in the summer. 'And you, you are not afraid?' I asked of Ma Sœur Courtés. 'Why should we be?' she replied simply. ' Hitherto none of our sisters have died, though one has been very ill and we have sent her to Algiers for change of air. But, if God willed to take us, we are quite ready; we should only go home a little sooner.' One could not but envy the bright, peaceful spirit which was thus willing to live on and work, or else to lie down and die, just as it should please God, without giving a thought to anything but the fulfilment of His will.

From Marengo the road becomes prettier every moment, winding through park-like grounds and wooded glades till we reached Zurich, having first forded the river Oued-el-Hachem, over which there is no bridge. This little town was built on the ruins of an old Roman city, and just after leaving its gates, we came upon a magnificent old Roman aqueduct with three tiers of arches in perfect preservation. Another hour's drive partly by the sea-shore, brought us to Cherchel itself, that Paradise of antiquarians! On all sides crop up Roman remains; beautiful capitals, magnificent marble pillars of breccia, porphyry and granite, red tufa walls, aqueducts, baths, temples, &c.

Cherchel was originally founded by some Phœnician colonists; then Juba II. embellished it and made it the capital of the kingdom of Mauritania under the name of Cæsarea; but Ptolemy, his son, having been assassinated, his kingdom was finally merged in the great Roman Empire. It afterwards became a favourite residence of the Emperor Theodosius and the seat of a bishopric; but was nearly destroyed by the Vandals at the time of their invasion of Africa. Above the town towers the beautiful peak of Ras-el-Amruch, called the 'Mamelon' by the French. Our first visit was to the museum; but though it contains some interesting statues, medals, and inscriptions, the most remarkable monuments have been transported to Algiers. Then we went to see the Great Mosque which has been converted into a military hospital; but the roof of which is supported by horse-shoe arches resting on eighty beautiful green granite columns forming part of an old Roman temple. Of the ancient Roman Palace, only some pillars with fine capitals remain : but the cisterns, which are of vast extent, still exist, with that wonderful durability which belongs only to Roman work; and still supply the town with water, as they did eighteen hundred years ago. From the baths, with their beautiful mosaic pavements, we wandered down to the sea-

shore which is covered with shells : and then across
some olive and orange groves, to what was the most
interesting thing to me in Cherchel—the ruins of the
Circus or amphitheatre, where the martyr St. Marcian
was devoured by wild beasts ; and where St. Severino
with his wife St. Aquila were burnt to death. The
seats round this Coliseum remain intact, as also the sub-
terranean chambers where the wild beasts were confined previous to being let out on their victims ; but the
centre of the arena has been planted with beans and
the whole place is sadly neglected. With the history
of these martyrs fresh in my mind, however, it was not
difficult to imagine and realise that scene of heroic
faith and courage. Further on, is another tomb like
the one we had seen the day before, only smaller.
This is supposed to have been built by Juba for his
retainers or freed slaves. Then we went to the theatre
where St. Arcadius was cut in pieces for confessing the
faith of Christ ; and so on to the port, where recent
excavations have discovered a variety of Roman vases
and curiosities, and among other things a vessel which
had evidently been submerged and was full of pottery.
There is nothing in the least interesting in the modern
town—only the everlasting barracks, 'Cafés,' and
' Billiards,' which seem to be necessities of French
existence in Algeria. So that having explored and
seen all that was worth looking at in the ancient

Cherchel, we started on our homeward route, this
time determining to take a new road which would
bring us to the railroad at El-Affroun, and so by
Blidah to Algiers. But it was a dreary journey, and,
as the evening closed in, the fatal mists rose with their
deadly miasma over the great plain which we were
slowly traversing, and we no longer wondered that our
good sisters' hospital at Marengo was so full.

Arrived at the station, we found on the platform a
poor man moaning and writhing in all the agonies
of ague fever and almost unconscious. We gave
him some oranges, which he eat whole and so rave-
nously that it seemed as if his thirst had become
unbearable. The poor fellow was returning to Blidah
where his mother was, from whom he had been
tempted by high wages to seek work in the plains—
only alas! to meet his death, it appeared; as at the
next station we saw him lifted out by the porters as if
all were over. That evening we returned to Algiers,
little thinking that in less than three months from that
time, a simultaneous Arab rising would have carried
fire and sword into the heart of the beautiful country
we had traversed, and that smoking homesteads and
charred and blackened forests would have replaced the
comfortable-looking farm buildings and smiling wood-
lands of the Mitidja!

After a few days' rest, we again hired our little

carriage ; but started this time in the opposite direction to visit the Kabyles in their own mountain homes. The correspondent of the 'Daily News,' in his late recital of the horrors which have been perpetrated in that part of the country since we were there, has familiarised our readers with both the scenery and people, and his descriptions are so accurate that I trust he will forgive my occasionally quoting his own words.

The dawn was just breaking as we drove out of Algiers through the suburbs of Mustapha Inférieur, past the race-course or 'Champ de Manœuvres,' meeting no one but a few Sisters of Charity on their way to early mass, or, here and there, a file of camels and their drivers slowly returning from the town to their desert homes. Great aloe hedges bordered the road, while here and there the ferula, with its flowery plume of golden blossoms and its graceful feathery leaves, was mingled with the spikey white flowers of the asphodel.

After about an hour's drive we reached the Maison Carrée or state prison, for a description of which I will quote the words of the above-mentioned correspondent.

'Maison Carrée is a prison, in which felons condemned to simple imprisonment are confined. It is a large square building, only one floor in height, enclosing 8,000 square mètres, or 80 acres of land, with a recreation yard and garden. It contains at the present time about 800 felons, of whom only 300 sleep in the prison, the remainder work out; some as far as 100 kilomètres distant. Of the 300 who sleep within the building from 60 to 70 are Europeans. The prisoners' uniform is of white linen; for the Europeans, it consists of trousers and blouse with a grey shashea or skull-cap, while the Arabs wear trousers cut short just below the knee, and a red and yellow shashea; the head dress of the severely punished is yellow. The building and its inhabitants are guarded by from 30 to 40 troops, and one warder, armed with a sword and gun, for every 30 prisoners. The dormitories are in a vaulted rectangular building, with ventilating windows in the roof. They are exceedingly close and unhealthy-looking, that occupied by the Arabs being about 30 mètres wide, $45\frac{1}{2}$ mètres long, and less than three mètres high. That occupied by the Europeans is much wider, but the same height and the same length. The want of pure air does not affect the Arabs much, for they are accustomed from their earliest childhood to breathe all manner of foulness, but the Europeans, notwithstanding that their dormitories are larger and less densely occupied, must suffer terribly; in fact, the inspector who accompanied me during my visit expressed himself very strongly on this point. Each prisoner is provided with a grass mat and a straw mattress. There is also a building set apart for old and infirm prisoners, and an infirmary

—a rectangular wooden construction, perhaps too well ventilated, containing from 60 to 70 beds. It is divided into two parts, with a room for the warder and servants in the centre. The door opens into this room, which is merely partitioned off on either side by wooden palings. As we entered, the division set apart for the Arabs was on our right, and that occupied by the Europeans on our left. Of the sick at that moment there were fourteen in all, of whom ten were Arabs, and the remaining four Europeans; the principal diseases from which they suffer are fever among the Europeans, and consumption among the Arabs. The living consists of two meals a day. In the morning the Arabs receive a bowl of soup, made of bread, beans, cabbages, rice, green vegetables and oil; while the Europeans receive the same mess, cooked in grease; at night the meal consists of beans and rice. They receive the same ration of bread as soldiers, and meat once a week. Besides this, they have the facility of buying different things at the canteen with the money they earn. Maison Carrée receives men condemned to any term of imprisonment above a year. There is one man suffering twenty years' imprisonment, and another fifteen years, while the remainder average from three to ten years. Among others there is a captain of Mobiles condemned to six years' imprisonment for having insulted his colonel. It is curious to

notice that the Arabs are principally suffering imprisonment for immoral conduct, there being comparatively
few cases of theft or homicide. The prisoners are
maintained by a contractor who feeds, clothes, and
doctors them, for which he receives from the Government 58 centimes per day per man. Besides this, he
has the power of letting out the men to farmers, and of
employing a certain number himself; but he is forced
to give each man he employs or lets out 20 centimes a
day. At the time I visited the prison he had 500 men
out of doors, who are guarded by a warder for every
twenty, as well as a certain number of soldiers.'

   After leaving the Maison Carrée, the road passes
through some richly-cultivated ground belonging to a
colony of Mahonnais, from the Spanish Isles, who are
supposed to be the first market gardeners in Europe.
They have built their village close to a famous spring
of water, from which the place is called 'Le Fort
d'Eau.' From thence we drove on through vineyards
and orchards to a large caravanseraï, close to which a
great market was going on, and hundreds of Arabs
were clustered together gesticulating and screaming in
a way worthy of 'ce peuple criard,' as Lamartine
calls them; while long files of camels and donkeys
marched alongside of us or were turned off to feed in
the adjoining pastures.

   Soon we came into a country of a far wilder

character, and stopped to bait at a village called the
'Col de Beni-Aïcha.' It was a wretched little post-
house; but the landlady quickly prepared some
luncheon for us in an arbour in the garden, and whilst
we were eating it, dilated on the misery of her position
without a church or a school for her children, and
exposed to constant fears of the rising of the Kabyles.
I have often wondered what became of those poor
people when that rising actually took place a month or
two later! From hence we at once entered into
Kabylia, the ground steadily rising till we came to the
top of the pass from whence we caught the first
beautiful view of the grand range of the Djurjura
Mountains, their rugged peaks glistening with snow.
Descending into the plain, which was full of large
storks feeding in the meadows, we crossed the Isser, a
fine broad river formed by the junction of two other
streams. Here we found a complete change in the
character and appearance of the inhabitants. Instead
of Arabs solemnly folded in their burnouses, sitting by
the roadside cafés or standing at their tent doors
doing nothing, we came upon laborious, patient plodding Kabyles toiling after their ploughs up the steep
sides of the hills (not one half acre of which was left
uncultivated), and with their bare shaved heads
forming the most wonderful contrast to the invariably
muffled-up Arabs. The Kabyle, in fact, is a totally

different animal. He hates a nomadic, roving life ; is
fond of his home, sober, inured to hard work, a careful
agriculturist, and full of intelligence in all industrial
arts and manufactures. In the National Exhibition at
Algiers every kind of fire-arms, daggers, ornaments,
tools, pottery, basket-work, &c., came from Kabylia,
besides a variety of different descriptions of cloth and
woollen goods. The Kabyles always reminded me of
the Russian peasants, in their singular aptitude for all
handicraft trades, and the patient, plodding perseverance with which they work. They are devoted to their
country, passionately attached to their mountain homes,
and hospitable and kind to strangers ; but, like the
Corsicans, nourish a never-dying vengeance against
any who have offended or ill-used them. They have
generally but one wife, and are fond of their children,
but women still occupy a very degraded position among
them. They do not live in tents, but in circular hay-
stack-looking thatched mud huts, sometimes without
roofs ; and generally with an enclosure of fine wattled
reeds round each hut, to keep in their cattle. They
fence their fields neatly with the same yellow reeds,
which grow in profusion by the river banks. I will
once more quote our Correspondent for a very accurate
description of this people and their habitations.

‘ The Kabyles are very mysterious in their way of
living ; thus almost all the houses in the village had a

KABYLE INTERIOR. KABYLE.

court-yard before them, with a doorway like a hurdle standing on one of its ends, through which it was impossible to see what was going on on the other side.

' I passed through the wicker-work doorway which I have already mentioned, into the courtyard, and entered the Kabyle house on the right. It was a building constructed of stones and mud, or rather clay; the walls were very thick, which was probably to keep out the heat, and had no windows. The roof, which was without a chimney, as is customary in Kabyle dwellings, was of long red roughly moulded tiles, shaped like cylinders split in two. The interior of the Kabyle house is divided into two parts, but the exterior has only one door, through which both the live stock and the family pass into the portion reserved to the latter; immediately on the left is a second doorway, beyond which is the cowshed, where the goats, sheep, mules, or donkeys, and horned cattle are placed at night. The living room looks more like a cellar than anything else; all round the walls are solid stone benches, less than a yard high, and about four feet broad, upon which the Kabyles sit or sleep on platted grass mats, which they make for that purpose. Against the walls, and on a sort of ledge above the cow-shed, were a number of large earthen jars, five feet high, in which the Kabyles keep their corn. These jars are made by the Kabyle women, one of whom stands in the middle and works at the inside while the others build up the jar on the outside. When it is finished the woman is lifted out and the jar is placed to dry in the sun or in the centre of a slow fire.

'Although the condition of the women is better in Kabylia than in the South of Algeria, it is nevertheless by no means enviable, for between the mule and the woman there is but little difference. The husband, or rather the master, is exceedingly jealous of his wife, or slave. The woman should never speak to any other man but her husband, and she should avoid as much as possible gazing on any other. To be received in the house of a Kabyle amongst his wives a man must be a bosom friend of long standing. Thus, when I asked to visit a Kabyle house at Tin-Cachin, the inhabitants made, first of all, some difficulty on account of the women, and it was only when they had been put out of the way that my request was complied with.

' The Kabyle costume consists of a long shirt reaching below the knees, a *burnous*, a white skull-cap, and a red *shashea* made of a woollen material. Some of the people wear shoes, but they generally take these off when they sit down, and only use them in the country to protect their feet against thorns, &c. The women wear a long chemise reaching to their ancles, fastened round the waist by a coloured sash, and a coloured handkerchief in their hair; many have bracelets round their wrists or ancles, earrings and ornaments in their hair, and some are tattooed about the face.'

After crossing the river we came to a Turkish castle, perched on a rock overhanging the stream, which was the scene of a sanguinary fight between the Kabyles and the Turks just before the French invasion. In fact, these people have never yet been conquered by any nation. They have only momentarily submitted to the French rule, and that from motives of self-interest, as they find a better market for their produce since the French occupation. The French Government also has wisely left them their own political organisation, which is as follows.[1] Every village is governed by a *Djemâa* or municipality. This *Djemâa* is composed of a president, a finance minister, and a certain number of councillors, who are to assist the president in his deliberations. These councillors are chosen from among what are called the *Kharoubas*, that is, each village is divided into so many houses inhabited by so many families. Those who are related to each other are formed into a *Kharouba* or tribe, and the said *Kharouba* selects its most intelligent or experienced members to represent the rest at the council. These men, called in Kabyle language *Enquals*, are

[1] This account is taken from the Reports of the *Bureaux Arabes* at Fort Napoléon and Tizi-Ozou, as inserted in the *Itinéraire de l'Algérie* by M. Louis Piesse.

held in the greatest consideration, and nothing is done without their advice and co-operation.

This Djemâa meets once a week, generally on a Friday evening, unless some extraordinary circumstance calls for more frequent gatherings. These assemblies, though noisy, are yet in reality far from disorderly. The Kabyle is used to political life, and has a great respect for law and authority. The judicial powers of the Djemâa are regulated by the established code called *Kanoun*; and in the administration of justice, these laws and those established by custom, or the *A da* of the country, are never departed from in the smallest particular.

The next village we came to was called *Taourga,* and is, curiously enough, inhabited almost entirely by a mixed race called *Konlourlis*, who are employed chiefly in leather-work and the embroidering of saddles and horse-trappings, of which we saw some very pretty specimens. *Tizi-Ozou,* which we reached soon after, is a pretty little town, with a large Turkish fortress built of Roman remains, which is now a stronghold of the French, and was the scene of one of the most important struggles of this year during the Kabyle revolt.

We only stopped to change horses and to look at the pretty little church on the green above the village, where there was Exposition of the Blessed Sacrament.

Then began the really picturesque and beautiful part
of our journey. We crossed twice the Oued-Sebaôu
(or River of Lions), which in some parts was very
deep, and then commenced the ascent to Fort Napoléon,
which is tremendously steep and long, although the
scenery is quite glorious. You wind up a magnificent
wooded gorge with a rushing stream below, while
above are the snowy peaks of the Djurjura Mountains,
as varied and beautiful in their shapes as those of the
Alps at St. Moritz. To the east is the rich and fertile
valley of Sebaôu, which divides the Kabyle country
into two parts; and beyond, the long line of sea coast
stretching from Dellis to Bougie; to the west, are the
deep ravines of the *Zouaoua*, with their jagged pointed
rocks and precipitous descents to the rushing torrents
below, the whole crowned by the glorious range of the
Djurjura. I have been a great deal in mountain
scenery, but I never saw anything more beautiful than
these Kabyle hills and gorges. No wonder the poor
fellows love their native land! Their villages are
generally perched on the very highest peak of each
separate hill, just as the Italian villages are and for the
same reason; i.e. to avoid sudden and unexpected
attacks from hostile tribes.

Fort Napoléon, or, as it is now called, *Le Fort
national*, is built in the centre of the warlike tribe of
the *Beni-Iraten* and on the site of a famous market-

place called in Kabyle language, *Souk-el-Arba.* It is
on a raised plateau 2,400 feet above the level of the
sea, but is itself commanded by the Kabyle villages
crowning the heights before-mentioned, which, in the
event of war, would make the place untenable should
the Kabyles possess cannon of long range. The so-
called fort is a space of twelve acres enclosed by a wall
twelve feet high flanked by seventeen bastions to
which there are only two entrances, one by the Algiers
and the other by the Djurjura gate. It boasts of one
street, which has private houses, or rather shops and
cafés on either side, a church, a presbytery, and the
convent and schools of the sisters of the 'Doctrine
Chrétienne.' The rest of the buildings consist of
barracks and officers' quarters, the latter perched on a
rising ground above the civilians' houses. It is looked
upon as a great *tour de force* that the carriage-road
from hence to Tizi-Ozou was made by the French
soldiers in twenty days, in spite of all the difficulties
caused by the steepness of the ascent, which compelled
them to resort to a perpetual zig-zag. But in the
making of good roads no country on earth equals the
French, and hence the rapidity of their communica-
tions. We found two very decent little rooms in an
inn close to the Tizi-Ozou or Algiers gate, kept
by an Alsatian and his wife who were very civil and
obliging.

I had a long talk the following morning with the good parish priest about the religious condition of the Kabyles. He said they were nominally Mahometans, but in reality had no religion at all. He considered that if the Government restrictions were removed, a great deal might be done towards Christianising them, but at present the Government positively forbids it, fearing thereby to exasperate the tribes. Several of the chiefs (and one especially who was highly considered among the Beni-Iraten) had sent to the ' Black Fathers ' to beg them to come to their villages to teach them and their children, but the authorities would not permit the priests to go. The fathers have learned medicine, and practise it constantly among the people, which gives them great hold and influence over them. There are both boys and girls in the sisters' schools, and the most intelligent among the boys are sent to the Archbishop's College. Yet those who have embraced Christianity have a good deal to suffer from their own people. The priest told me that one of the lads whom I saw had been driven out of his home by his own mother because he confessed to having been baptised in the faith of Christ. But this opposition would probably cease if the chiefs were themselves to be converted.

After breakfast we procured horses from the Commandant and rode towards the Col de Tivordat, a

beautiful wild ride, for a description of which I will
quote once more our ' Daily News' Correspondent :—

' The road runs towards the north, and, after crossing
the valley, winds through the hills for the entire
distance. At times it is tolerably open on either side ;
at others it is cut in the massive rock, which rises up
above your head on either side ; at others, again, it
passes for a considerable distance at the edge of a deep
ravine, at the bottom of which runs a little stream. At
this point horsemen are obliged to advance in Indian
file ; and if a horse were to take it into his head to
dance about, both he and his rider would in all proba-
bility roll to the bottom of the precipice. But this is
of very rare occurrence, for the Arab horse is as sure-
footed as the mule—he will go anywhere and climb
anything. At times the road was like stone steps, and
so steep that a man would have had to climb on his
hands and feet ; but our horses went up it without any
difficulty, and without it being necessary to urge them
to the work in the slightest degree. All that was
necessary was to catch hold of a tress of the horse's
mane, give him his head, and he picked his way up the
most difficult paths in the cleverest manner imaginable.
All along the road we came upon fields of barley, notwithstanding the apparent barrenness of the soil.
There were besides the olive and fig trees—a continual
source of wealth to the Kabyle—and gigantic wild

vines climbing up everything. We passed through several villages, and caught sight of a great many others perched upon the summit of the hills.'

On our return we stopped at the Kabyle village of Sharetan, where the chief came up to where I was sketching and begged us to pay them a visit in their homes. We found them miserably dirty and dark, with no furniture save certain great pots for holding corn and water, which stood in one corner of the hut. But in almost all the women were weaving white stuff for burnouses on roughly-constructed looms, and it seemed incredible how such beautiful fine clean material could come out of such unpromising looking workshops. The women themselves, and especially the children, were wonderfully handsome, with glorious dark eyes, pensive and somewhat dreamy faces of an oval shape, and beautiful hands and arms. Their skins were dark but clear, and the only thing that spoiled their beauty to European eyes was their habit of tattooing the marks of their tribe on their forehead or chins ; some had a cross, and others palm leaves thus indelibly engraved upon them. Unlike the Arabs, the Kabyle women have their faces uncovered. They were loaded with native ornaments, some very beautiful and curious in form, with precious stones or coral roughly inlaid in them. Their haïks were fastened with silver pins of a peculiar shape and of fine workmanship, connected with a chain, and they wore two or three pairs of earrings one over the other (some put through the upper part of the ear and others through the lower), with a profusion of bracelets and necklaces. The shapes of their pottery also were most picturesque, and the colour a peculiar kind of brown.

In the evening we went to dine with the commandant, Colonel Herson, and his wife, and on our arrival found her in a perfect agony at his non-appearance. ' He had gone to meet us,' she said, 'and had not yet returned ;' adding that she lived in continual terror of the Kabyles waylaying and murdering him. We could not help sympathising in her anxiety, which, however, was relieved after about an hour by the appearance of the colonel in person, who had somehow lost his way in the hills. But it was impossible not to feel for this poor little Parisian lady, so pretty, bright, and young, in fact scarcely more than a bride, suddenly transported to this out-of-the-way fortress, where there was no society whatever, and no *distraction* of any kind, her husband away all day on often perilous service ; and only two other ladies in the place, with neither of whom she was at all intimate. She told us that even her maid had left her, being unable to bear the *ennui*. She added that she was very fond of music, but that no piano could be brought such a distance and up such a steep ascent ; and as she had no children, and could get scarcely any books, I cannot conceive a more dull and wearisome life ! There was also great difficulty in getting any variety of food, or any but soldier servants, the best of whom had gone with their regiments to the war ; so that her position altogether was most dismal.

The next morning we started on a long expedition to *Ait-l'Hassen,* a Kabyle village on the top of one of the mountains, about ten miles from Fort Napoléon, on the left bank of the Oued Beni-Aïssi, and inhabited by the tribe of the Beni-Yenni, who are renowned all over the country for their manufacture of arms and jewels. We had capital mules, and accomplished the journey in about four hours, though the roads were terribly steep and bad, and M—— preferred walking a great part of the way. On crossing the river one of our mules fell in the deep and rapid part of the current, but fortunately its rider escaped with a wetting. The path wound down the side of one mountain and up the next by an almost inaccessible track, but our poor beasts were wonderfully sure-footed and did not slip, though it was like climbing up the side of a house. We stopped outside the town, in a beautiful grove of old olive trees, to eat our luncheon, and found that it formed part of the burial-ground of the tribe of Beni-Yenni, though only a stone here and there served to mark the spot where each lay in his grassy bed. We

L

had not been there long when the Kadi of the village came to insist on our coming up to his house, where we found a magnificent feast prepared for us, in a square whitewashed room spread with carpets. Great bowls of the universal 'cous-cous,' lamb and chickens cooked with rice in a kind of pilau and covered with grease, were spread before us, together with large jars of sour milk, the Kabyles' favourite beverage. Fortunately, we could plead having previously eaten, and I, that my religion precluded my eating meat in Lent, and the latter excuse was readily accepted, though we were compelled to swallow some of the hated 'cous-cous,' so as not altogether to disappoint and thwart their hospitality. Then the sheik introduced us to his wife, who was accompanied by her sister and cousins, some of whom were very handsome and covered with jewels, but abominably painted. We in vain tried to purchase some of their ornaments, but they replied, 'If we were to sell them, we should no longer belong to our husbands.' They showed us the circular brooches given to them by their lords and masters when they gave birth to a male child. Some are flat, with coral and green enamel let in, and others are with knobs set in a circle.

These poor women are regularly *bought* in fact, the ordinary price being from 200 to 300 francs; but the pretty ones are much dearer. They do all the hard work, carry wood and water, labour in the fields, grind the corn, and weave the stuff that forms their burnouses and haïks. The labour of bringing the water from the deep ravines and gorges below up to the very tops of these hills is something fearful, and the water, even when brought, is brackish and bad. They are married at thirteen and fourteen, and by dint of toil and ill-usage become old women at thirty. But they have some of the finer elements of a mountain race, and often accompany their husbands to war. We were disappointed not to find any manufactory of their curious and characteristic jewellery, but they seem all to be made by individuals at home. Their earrings were so massive and heavy that they are compelled to wear them with a circle round the ear, and their pins for the haïks are beautiful in shape and design ; but, as I said before, we could not persuade them to part with any, and those we afterwards procured from Dorez' famous curiosity shop in Algiers, though quaint and pretty, were not equal to those we saw worn by the peasants themselves. We also tried in vain to see the making of the Kabyle pots. They declared they had none in stock, though the shapes of those they used were so beautiful that one longed to draw each one.

We returned by another and a shorter route, crossing this time another river called the Oued-Djenn, and passing through the most lovely gorge we had

yet seen. The ground was carpeted with white heath
in full blossom, beautiful orchids, wild lavender and
rosemary, cistus both white and lilac, and every
description of aromatic shrub. Then, we came to an
olive wood, through which we rode for an hour,
continually ascending, till we arrived at a picturesque
fountain, shaded by cork trees, round which a multitude of young girls who had been employed in gathering the olive berries were clustered, watering their
mules. One of them, a child of fifteen, had the most
perfectly beautiful face I ever saw, and she was
evidently conscious of it, and treated with a kind of
deference by her companions. Then we came into a
new and smoother road lately made by the French
across the valley, and galloped on towards the Fort,
the sunset gilding the peaks of the Djurdura with
those wonderful tints which none but those who have
been in Africa can imagine. On our way we had had
an amusing conversation with our little Kabyle guide,
the owner of one of the mules, who appeared to us a
child ; but he gravely informed us that he was fifteen,
and already married, and proceeded to give us an
account of the music and festivities which had taken
place on the occasion. He had been educated at a
French Kabyle school, which had been opened
during the last few years by the French Government,
at Fort Napoléon, and in which the boys are taught

every kind of trade. Colonel Herson told me that their intelligence and quickness were wonderful, and that though the school would only hold 200 children, there were upwards of 400 applicants for admission.

The following day we took leave of our kind friends at the Fort, and returned by the same route to Algiers, which we reached after a journey of thirteen hours, thoroughly delighted with our expedition. Before closing this chapter on the Kabyles, I will give an extract from an unpublished MS. written in 1847 by M. le Comte Ernest De Stackelberg on this singular people, giving the most concise and accurate description of them which I have yet met with.

'The Berbers or Kabyles are the result of a fusion between the Aborigènes (who were immigrants of Canaanitish origin) and the people who succeeded them in the domination of Algeria, and principally of the Vandals, who were all powerful in this country from 438 to 534. On the occasion of the great Arab invasion, the Kabyles retired into their mountain fastnesses; and although nominally embracing Islamism, contrived to maintain their independence, which is one of the causes of the hatred which has always existed between them and the Arabs. On no single occasion have they ever submitted to the Turks, who were, on the contrary, compelled to pay a kind of quit-money for passing through their territory when they went to raise taxes from the Arab tribes. It appears, however, that they must have, more or less, submitted to the Roman yoke, as, even in their most distant and in-accessible valleys, we find ruins which attest the presence of that great and wonderful people.

'The Kabyle language differs entirely from that spoken by the Arabs. They are laborious, good agriculturists, and clever in manufactures, especially of linen and woollen stuffs. They live a sedentary life, have flourishing villages, and roofed and whitewashed houses. When they have no work at home, they go down to the towns to earn money, for their thirst for gold is equal to that of the Arabs. But their hatred of strangers soon drives them back to their mountain homes. No aristocracy is recognised by the Kabyles. Their form of government is democratic, and even the chiefs of their tribes have little power. On the other hand, the influence of the Marabouts is supreme.

'The Kabyles are spread over all the three provinces of Algeria. Those of the Atlas and in the neighbour-hood of Blida (like the Beni-Moussa, the Mouzaïa, &c.) are now subject to France, and in consequence of their vicinity to Algiers, even consented occasionally to pay tribute to the Turks. Two of the most important branches of the Kabyle race, in fact, inhabit the province of Algiers: to the west, they occupy all the space between the Chélif and the sea; to the east, what is called "La Grande Kabylie," which forms a triangle, the point of which is at Sétif, and the base rests on the seashore from Dellis to Collo. The first of these has been the scene of fierce struggles between the French and themselves. Here was the barbarous stifling in the grotto : and the natives, hunted, tracked and impoverished, yielded from sheer exhaustion to their conquerors, but with an undying hatred in their hearts which subsequent events may develop.

'As to the "Grande Kabylie," it is in a great measure a *terra incognita* to the French, and the very name causes them to hesitate before undertaking any serious expedition against them.

' It is fair to add that as the Kabyles are in no way aggressive, and never fight save when their own territory is invaded, they need in no way interfere with the aggrandisement of French influence around them. Their position may be hostile, but it is the hostility of neutrals, unless directly attacked.

' All I have now said applies to the Kabyles, properly so called, who reside in the Tell of Algeria. In the south of the province of Constantine, and on the confines of the Desert, are a tribe of these very people who are nomads and shepherds, who live in tents like the Arabs, and have all the external appearance of the latter. These are the tribe of the *Chaouyas,* who yet are of Kabyle or Berber origin, and speak the Kabyle language with very little variety. But, less happy than their brethren in the mountains, these Kabyles have remained in the plains, and have not been able to maintain their independence. They are not warlike, or rich ; and in some cases have even consented to pay tribute to France.

'But there is again another Kabyle tribe, the *Biscris*, living (as their name implies) at Biskra and other parts of the Desert, under the shadow of the palms and in the oases which are scattered all along the edge of the Sahara. They are so transformed by their desert lives as to be almost impossible to distinguish from the Arabs, unless it be through their darker tint, which they owe to frequent mixture with the negroes of central Africa. These Biscris may occasionally be met with in the large towns, where they act as porters and water carriers, but their home is in the sandy desert, and their heart is thoroughly Kabyle.'

KABYLE BROOCH GIVEN ON THE BIRTH OF A BOY.

CHAPTER VI.

CONSTANTINE.

MY horror of the sea had made me hope to escape any further voyages till we were compelled to return to Europe; and I therefore intended to have gone to Constantine, either over the mountains beyond Fort Napoléon ; or else by Aumale and Sétif, taking the diligence from the latter place. But already the insurrection was brewing ; various skirmishes had taken place at Sétif and its neighbourhood, and my kind old friend the Admiral of the port received such alarming accounts of the state of the country, and of the risks to travellers on those comparatively unfrequented roads, that I did not dare expose M—— to the chance of being made a Kabyle prisoner. So, very reluctantly, I took berths on board the 'Hermes,' whose Captain, a most gentlemanlike French officer, was a great friend of Admiral La Maurelle's. What I did not know, however, till too late, was, that this 'Hermes' goes by the name of

'Le Grand Rouleur,' among the coasting ships of the
'Messageries Impériales'—being so narrow and long
that she pitches even in the stillest water!

My usual bad luck at sea awaited me. The admiral
had kindly taken us on board in his beautiful barque,
in which we had already made some delightful expeditions. And the signal for departure had been long
since telegraphed from the Admiralty Stairs, but still
we tossed helplessly and hopelessly in the bay. At
last, the captain came up to me to say that the weather
was so rough outside that he should not steam out of
harbour before the following day, and advised us to
return on shore. So we were again landed, sulkily
enough, and on returning to our comfortable apartment
found it already occupied by a fresh family, and had to
breakfast disconsolately in the coffee room with our
worldly goods piled up alongside of us, too cross to go
and see our friends from whom we had so lately parted
and hating the sea more than ever in our hearts! I
consoled myself by going to a meeting of the 'Mères
Chrétiennes,' who were having a public retreat at the
Jesuit Church, which was preached by a very eloquent
Father of the society; and towards evening we again
embarked in a heavy sea and clambered up the sides of
our prison which, this time, got under weigh about four
o'clock in the morning. I spare my readers the
description of our miseries for the next few days.

Everyone was ill; and even when it ceased to blow, the swell only increased our discomfort. Owing to the gale we did not arrive at Dellis till eleven on Sunday morning. But as we were to stay there some few hours to take in cargo, I gladly landed and got to church, finding also the Sisters of the 'Doctrine Chrétienne,' who had a beautiful house and schools there, and are universally beloved by the people. Dellis is a bright little town, built on the ruins of an old Roman city, with hanging gardens and vineyards above, remarkable for a peculiar kind of white grape which is a great favourite in Algiers. A fine 'koubba,' of some Mahometan Saint, stands on a rising ground overhanging the place; and we were told of some curious Roman cisterns, which we had not time, however, to visit.

Our next landing-place was Bougie; a beautiful old town, built on the borders of the gulf of the same name, and under the shadow of the grand old mountain of Gouraïa, which rises more than two thousand feet above the level of the sea. To the east is the Cape Carbon, formed of a great mass of bare red rocks, one of which, looking like a huge sugar loaf, seems as if it were detached from the point, and being hollowed into a natural arch by the action of the water, serves as a shelter for the fishermen's boats. To this arch the tradition is attached that it was once the place of concealment of the famous Raymond Lulli, when he came to Africa, in the thirteenth century, to strive to convert the Mussulmen. He had been successful at Bôna and along the coast, where his venerable appearance and earnestness had won the universal respect of the inhabitants; but, on his arrival at Bougie, the Mahometans rose against him and stoned him. Wounded and mangled, he crept into this arch to hide himself, where he was found and rescued by some Genoese sailors; but he only lived long enough to come in sight of his native Island of Majorca, when he expired of his wounds on the deck of their vessel.

A very curious old Saracenic fort remains close to the little pier, where we gladly landed, and walked up the steep street till we came to a magnificent palm tree, under which Arabs were squatted in solemn rows. From thence, we toiled up still higher, past the church, and so on to the beautiful old kasba built by Peter of Navarre in 1509; and though its towers have been partly destroyed by succeeding invaders, it is still a magnificent pile of buildings, from whence there is a glorious view of the bay and the town below. There is a fine forest behind the kasba reaching up to the lower spurs of the mountains through which the walks and drives are said to be lovely. But unfortunately the waning light prevented our pushing our explorations any further. Bougie was founded by Augustus thirty-

three years before Christ; but eight years later he gave
this African province to Juba II., king of Mauritania,
in exchange for the states which he had incorporated
with the Roman Empire. A multitude of old inscriptions corroborate the fact. Then Bougie fell into the
hands of the Vandals, who made it their capital until
the seizure of Carthage. Its ancient name was Saldæ,
and it was the seat of a bishopric. In 484, one of its
most eminent bishops assisted at the Council of
Carthage convoked by Huneric. Bougie then passed
through a succession of Mahometan rulers, and, afterwards, fell into the hands of the Spaniards and became
a great commercial centre; exporting every kind of
grain, wool, leather, oil, and above all wax; hence
its present name.

When we returned to the 'Hermes,' about one
hundred and fifty Arabs came on board with us, and
rolled themselves up on the deck in different positions,
as it was impossible to stand from the violence of the
swell.

Djidjelli was the next place where we stopped to
take in cargo. It is built on a rocky peninsula, connected by a narrow isthmus with the main land; and
its ancient history is identical with that of Bougie. It
is famous for its olives, which are grafted far more
carefully than in other parts of Algeria. Here two
hundred troops were embarked, bound for Collo; they

brought uncomfortable accounts of the general rising
of the tribes near Sétif, and seemed to think they should
have 'sharp work' soon; which prediction was speedily
verified. We had a very intelligent man on board, the
agent of a rich French colonist, who was on his way to
buy cattle at Constantine. He confirmed all I had heard
at Algiers of the difficulties of the labour question, and
evidently hoped more from the importation of Alsatians
than from emigrants from England or other countries.
But still his cry was the same as the rest: 'Il ne nous
manque que des bras!' Soon we arrived at Collo,
where the heavy swell prevented our landing, to my
great disappointment. The coast was very fine,
backed by beautiful mountains, and one especially, of a
conical shape, was richly wooded. A little further on
is a perpendicular red rock, rounded at the top and one
hundred and eighty feet high, standing out by itself
like a little island, and covered with every variety of
sea bird, which were perched in hundreds on the
ledges and holes of the rocks. It reminded me of
Handa Island, off Scourie in Sutherlandshire, where I
had so often watched such myriads of these birds,
whose nests honeycombed the whole surface of the
cliffs. A succession of these rocky islands stand out
all along the coast, till you arrive at the Stora lighthouse: where we joyfully left our rolling steamer, and
landed in a small boat in a pelting shower, leaving the

luggage to follow us to Philippeville. There are plenty of little carriages at Stora to take passengers on to the latter port, which is five miles off; and nothing can be more beautiful than the drive, which runs between the sea shore and the wooded mountains and ravines which form the back ground of this fine coast.

Our first arrival at Philippeville was inauspicious, as every inn was full. But at last the good landlady of the 'Orient' undertook to find us two little rooms 'au troisième,' which did very well for one night. Nearly 60,000*l.* have been expended by the French Government in striving to make a good harbour at Philippeville, in which they have not yet succeeded; as the storms on that coast are almost like Indian cyclones, and it is calculated that nearly two millions' worth of francs are annually sunk in these waters from the multiplicity of wrecks!

There is nothing in the least interesting in the modern town, save a great establishment of the Sisters of the 'Doctrine Chrétienne,' who have twenty-seven sisters at work here and upwards of one thousand children. The 'rouges' have left them in peace, contenting themselves with scribbling 'Liberté, Égalité, et Fraternité' in large letters over their gates. We took a beautiful walk on the ramparts above the town, which command a glorious view of the bay, and the island of Srigina—but had not sufficiently recovered

from our rough passage to visit the Museum or the
ancient cisterns, which we were afterwards told contained some interesting Roman remains. Philippeville,
the ancient *Rusicade*, is honourably mentioned in Ecclesiastical history as the seat of an important bishopric.
Verulus, one of its bishops, who assisted at the Council
of Carthage in 260, was martyred by the schismatics ;
while Faustinius, a century later, confirmed the faith
for which his predecessor had shed his blood, and was
mainly instrumental in the condemnation of the
Donatist heresy and its suppression in the North of
Africa. The history of the African Church, is it not
one continued series of struggles and martyrdoms ?

That afternoon we started by the new railroad for
Constantine, which we reached safely after a journey
of five or six hours, although we were afterwards told
that it was the most dangerous line in existence and
that accidents were almost of daily occurrence ! The
railroad certainly winds in the most eccentric way,
through beautiful mountains, in a series of zigzags and
sharp curves, like an Alpine carriage-road, every
moment getting higher and higher till you come to the
region of snow. Then the road dips a little ; and to
the right, in the valley below, a smiling little village
appears, with palm trees and orchards, which is a
favourite watering place of the inhabitants of Constantine. Tradition asserts that lions still frequent this

neighbourhood; but we failed to come across any during our stay.

I never saw any place the position of which struck me as so magnificent as that of Constantine, and the longer we stayed there the more I admired it. It is built on a high plateau, forming a peninsula, round three sides of which rushes a rapid river, called the Roumel, at a depth of upwards of a thousand feet, emptying itself to the south in a succession of beautiful cascades. There is only one point by which the place is in any way accessible—where a natural arch seems thrown over the abyss (which is edged with pointed rocks), at a height which makes one dizzy to look at. Over this side of the river a bridge called El-Kantra has been thrown, connecting the town with the mainland; but it seems incredible how the French could ever have taken possession of a place so impregnable both by nature and art.

Constantine, like Algiers, is divided into two distinct towns, of which I need not say that the Arab is the only one which is interesting; but that has a *cachet* peculiarly its own. The streets are excessively narrow, with curious projecting buttresses, widening towards the top, so that they almost meet overhead. Its native inhabitants number upwards of thirty thousand souls; and Constantine is besides the great centre of commerce for all the Arabs of the interior.

M

As in almost all Oriental towns, the different trades live each in their separate quarters. There is one for shoemakers, another for workers in leather (the largest manufacture in the place), some of which is beautifully embroidered ; another for jewellers, and so on for bakers, butchers, and all other trades. In those curious narrow, tortuous passages, and heaped up behind those little dark stalls, are untold treasures in gold and silver, exquisite stuffs, and every description of arms and saddlery. Yet it is only after a cup of coffee and a good deal of preliminary conversation that you can induce the vendors, squatted solemnly by the side of their tempting wares, to exert themselves in the least to show or sell you anything. They seem utterly indifferent to the sale of their goods, and you have to hunt up each article for yourself. But there is a fascination in these little streets (some of which are entirely covered over, as in Cairo) which made us return to them again and again during our stay.

We found very comfortable rooms at the Hôtel d'Orient, and the best *table-d'hôte* in Algeria, which is saying a good deal where all are good.

Our first visit was to the cathedral, which was formerly the mosque of Souk-er-Rezel, and of which the beautiful marble columns, coloured tiles, arabesques, and richly worked 'nimbar' still remain. The venerable Bishop, Las Casas, had lately resigned his bishopric, in consequence of ill-health, and no successor had yet been appointed. Poor man! He undertook various extensive works trusting to the promises of the Emperor and Empress; then came the downfall of the Imperial dynasty, and with it of all his hopes. The pressure of money difficulties brought on brain fever, and the doctors at last declared that his only chance of life was in giving up altogether his pastoral charge.

After seeing the cathedral, the mayor or prefect of the town, to whom we had letters of introduction, most good-naturedly came to escort us to the cascades—the most beautiful drive in the neighbourhood of Constantine. We found that this gentleman was a native of Palermo, so that we soon discovered plenty of subjects of common interest. Crossing the little 'place,' which was crowded with mules and camels, and passing by the gate of Bab-el-Oued, called by the French 'De la Vallée,' you come first to the great native market, held in a large enclosed space just outside the principal entrance to the town; then to a kind of public garden, where a good many ancient statues and columns have been removed from the museum: and then, turning sharply to the right, you descend by a steep path to some flour-mills near a thermal spring, which are placed just at the mouth of the beautiful ravine of the Roumel. Above your head towers the tremendous rock called Sidi Rached, forming the extreme southern point of the town and adjoining the Kasba. This is the Tarpeian Rock of Constantine, from whence the Beys used to precipitate their criminals, and especially their wives, if suspected of infidelity. Winding by a narrow path under this rock you come to a succession of magnificent waterfalls, and above them a gigantic natural arch spanning the whole space above the river, and that at such a height, that it makes one's neck ache to look up. The waters of the Roumel here fall in three separate gradations and then disappear and are lost in the rock, to reappear again both above and below. Fortunately for us the water was low; so that we could scramble from stone to stone up the bed of the torrent and see to perfection not only this first wonderful arch, spanning the space from the Kasba to the Sidi Meçid, but also three other arches further on, thrown, as it were, across the river; while the surrounding rocks were honeycombed with birds'-nests, and hundreds of crows, storks and other birds were flying in and out, looking like specks from where we stood feeling like very pigmies in the midst of a scene of such intense natural grandeur.

In the little pools caused by the receding of the water, Arab tanners were preparing their hides, or washing their clothes. On one of the precipitous rocks to the right is a Latin inscription recording the

CASCADE. CONSTANTINE

martyrdom of Marino and Jacob, with their companions, gardeners, who had the courage to die for their
faith, after having undergone unheard of tortures at
Cirta (the ancient Constantine) in the year 259.
M. de Cherbonneau is anxious for a chapel to be
built on or near this spot, and writes :—

'Would it not be well thus to prove to the native
population that the religion of Christ reigned in
Constantine before that of Mahomet, and that we have
as much respect and devotion for our saints as they
have for their marabouts ?'

After lingering some time in this magnificent gorge,
the prefect took us into a beautiful valley, through a
succession of orange and citron groves, to a point
where we obtained a still more picturesque view of the
cascades. A pretty Swiss cottage had been built a
little higher up, occupied by the Chasseurs d'Afrique;
and nothing could be a greater contrast to the stern
grandeur of the rugged ravine we had so lately left
than the smiling, flowery gardens and orchards of this
little glen, at the bottom of which a branch of the
Roumel was swiftly and silently running, overshadowed
by peach and almond trees in full blossom.

Reascending the steep hill which led to the town, we
turned to the left to see the French and Arab ceme-
teries, each enclosed by their cactus and aloe hedges,
and which are very nicely kept. All day, from our

little inn, we had watched the long funeral processions
of the Arabs passing through the Bab-el-Oued gate,
on their way to this cemetery, chanting in a low monotonous voice, and bearing the bodies of their dead, not
in coffins, but laid on tressels and covered with green
embroidered cloths, the richness of which varied with
the rank of the deceased. From thence we drove past
the conflux of the Roumel and Bou-Merzoug till we
came to a beautiful old Roman aqueduct, part of
which is still in perfect preservation. It has five
circular stone arches, upwards of sixty feet high, and
formerly conveyed the water from the hills to the
town. The view from hence of this side of Constantine, with its tanneries and circular mud beehives, is
most curious. Certainly it is a marvellous place!
Well may it be called by the Arabs ' Belad-el-Haoua '
(the City of the Air). It is rather like Ronda as to
its position, and seems as it were suspended at the top
of those high cliffs, which render it, as I have before
said, inaccessible save on the east side. The great
limestone rocks rise in sheer precipices on either side
of the ravine, and the storks, solemnly flapping their
great wings as they leave the walls to fish in the
torrent below, seem to be the only living things willing
to face the abyss.

In the afternoon, one of the officers on the general's
staff, Colonel Cervelle, whose relations we had known

at Algiers, very kindly volunteered to lionise us over
the town, and first took us to the palace of the Bey,
which is in a 'place' behind the cathedral, and is now
occupied as the head-quarters of the general in command of the town, and also of the 'Bureau Arabe,' the
nature of which office I shall explain later. This
palace, which brings to one's mind the pictures in the
'Arabian Nights,' is in the Moorish style, but chiefly
remarkable for its three gardens enclosed in the centre
of each of the three quadrangles of which the building is composed, surrounded by galleries beautifully
coloured and painted, from whence you look down on
a mass of orange and citron trees and beautiful flowers.
The frescoes on the walls of these galleries are most
original and quaint, representing naval combats with
ridiculous ships and boats, and cannon a good deal
bigger than either; but the Mussulman tradition is
rigorously adhered to, the cannon being supposed to
be fired by invisible hands, as no figures are represented. From thence we went to the museum, which
contains a very interesting collection of ancient pottery,
arms, jewellery and medals; but the most beautiful
thing is a bronze statue of a 'Winged Victory,' twenty-
three inches high, discovered under the old Kasba
during the excavations made there in 1858. There
are also specimens of the various minerals and
products of the province : among others, a species

of salt like deep yellow alabaster. The *Chaouc* of
the mayor obtained a specimen of this yellow spar-
looking substance for me, and told us that it was
brought from Milah, a village near Constantine, on the
road to Sétif, and that it was dug out of a rock called
Radgusie : but I could not ascertain if any use was
made of this salt in their trades.

From the museum we clambered up to the Kasba,
which from the time of the Romans has been the
stronghold of the possessors of Constantine. It is
placed on the highest point to the south of the town,
and beneath are the deep ravines of the Roumel.
The view from the battlements and ramparts is
quite glorious, looking over the fertile and beautiful
plains which extend from the town to the range of
mountains beyond. It was the scene of a tremendous
struggle with the Arabs at the time of the French
invasion, and hundreds of men, women and children
precipitated themselves over the walls into the ravine
below, sooner than fall into the hands of the conquerors.
A column in the centre of the principal square records
the names of the officers and men who fell in that
sanguinary fight. A multitude of very curious old
Roman inscriptions have been discovered on this spot,
and let into the walls, recording the glories of the
ancient Cirta (Constantine), which had been the
capital of Jugurtha's kingdom of Numidia, and was

transformed into a Roman colony by Julius Cæsar, who justly looked upon it as the key of the whole country. The Kasba has little else left of interest, as it has been completely rebuilt by the French, who have converted it into three separate barracks, for the infantry, artillery, and engineers. But in one corner they have constructed a beautiful military hospital, which is under the care of the Sisters of St. Vincent of Paul, Ma Sœur Tivollier being the Superior, and universally beloved and respected by both officers and men. They have sixteen Sisters at work there at this moment, and upwards of five hundred sick and wounded. Every day fresh victims were brought in from the seat of the insurrection, which was then becoming serious in the neighbourhood of Sétif.

Wearied with our sight-seeing, we gladly left the Kasba and strolled again into the curious old Arab quarter, which was a never-ending scene of amusement and interest. This time we threaded a narrow passage just behind our hotel, the first part of which was occupied exclusively by cook-shops. Then we came to one of those curious old Moorish horseshoe-shaped doors with big head nails, and pushing it open, came into a court, round which were a number of little rooms in which were squatted the weavers of burnouses and haïks. It is estimated that upwards of thirty thousand burnouses and sixty thousand haïks are annually woven in Constantine alone. But there is every kind of variety and price. The dearest and most beautiful are the *gandouras*, which are a mixture of silk and wool, and nearly as fine as muslin; they are only worn by the higher classes. But there are an infinite number of other kinds, some white, some striped, some black, and some (the *bidi*) are entirely grey or a soft mouse colour. These are immensely thick, and worn chiefly by the mountaineers, as they keep out any amount of wet or cold.

The haïks are made in looms, like the *tellis* for the tents, six or eight persons working at each at a time. But the difficulty here as elsewhere was to get the weavers to sell any. Their work was generally done to order, they had no stock, and it was only after a great deal of mysterious intercourse between the weavers and our guide (the *Chaouc* before named) that we obtained a gandoura and a haïk, and both at very high prices. Leaving the burnous court, we walked on to the shoe bazaar, where every description of bright-coloured shoe and slipper was being embroidered; and so out by a curious old double gate which opens inwards so as to mask the entrance to a small square where camels were resting with their little ones, close to a picturesque fountain. Here a Dervish with long hair and tattered clothes was praying and begging at the same time, and there a tanner was spreading out

sheets of bright crimson leather to dry.   Storks were
perched on the top of all the principal houses in the
Arab quarter, and big vultures swooped down over the
town from time to time, being, in fact, the only real
scavengers of the place.   We lingered by this old gate,
looking down on this curious scene, till warned by the
fading light that we must hurry home if we would not
be altogether lost in those tortuous streets.   But it is
impossible to describe in words the beauty of the
different groups, or the picturesqueness of these Eastern
bazaars and their quaint surroundings; Lewis alone
can paint them in all their minute details.

The following day we resolved to devote to the
mosques, which are very numerous and curious.   Nor
is this to be wondered at, when we recollect the excessive
devotion of the population, and the presence among
them of so large a number of religious sects or confraternities, who have made Constantine their head-
quarters.

The first we went to was in the principal street, close
to the 'place' of El-Betha.   It has been built on the
ruins of a Pagan temple, and M. Cherbonneau has
found various curious inscriptions proving that it must
have been originally a pantheon; for one refers to a
Temple of Venus, another to the Goddess of Concord,
while on the base of one of the pedestals is an inscription recording the name of the Roman questor who

erected it. Outside there is nothing to be seen but a
high wall pierced with one or two semi-circular holes
for light ; but the inside presents the usual features of
an outer court and arched colonnades leading to the
mosque itself, which is divided into five naves, corresponding with the five doors, with forty-seven columns.
But the whole has been modernised, white-washed and
spoiled. Far different is that of Djama Sidi El-
Kettani, built by Salah Bey, which is in the Place
Négrier, a triangular space just above the most picturesque of the Arab quarters, planted with trees, and
with a fountain in the centre, while on three sides are
Jewish curiosity-shops of various kinds, jewellers,
vendors of arms, and saddlery, &c. Once a week there
is an amusing auction of old clothes here, in which
every variety of curious stuffs and dresses may be procured, provided you are not too particular as to their
previous wearers.

The entrance to the mosque is by a great iron-
clamped door, which opens into a beautiful staircase
of black and white marble. On the black half of the
said stairs the faithful alone may walk ! At the top
of the staircase you come into a white marble court,
round which is a carved gallery. The minaret rises on
the opposite side, but out of this court are two beautifully carved doors leading into the mosque. On
entering, the first thing which strikes the eye is an

exquisite *mihrab* or praying place, a niche richly
festooned with arabesques and supported by four
marble columns.   Here the Iman prostrates himself in
prayer, turned towards Mecca and the East.   The
shape of this mosque is a long square ; the ceiling is
boarded, each plank being coloured alternately red and
green, with beautiful designs of roses and flowers
painted on them.   White marble columns divide the
naves and support the cupolas, while coloured tiles of
an infinite variety of patterns cover the walls.   But the
glory of the whole is the *nimbar* or pulpit, in which
every description of rare agate or marble is introduced.

Adjoining this mosque is the *medersa* or college, also
built by Salah Bey, where about twenty ecclesiastical
students are maintained at the cost of their respective
tribes.   In the Mahometan system, the temporal power
is strictly bound up with the spiritual ; for the Koran
is not only a religious guide, but a civil and political
code which regulates the relations of men to each other
and serves as the mechanism of Mussulman society.
The tombs of Salah and his family are placed at the
bottom of the court, in a small recess railed off from the
rest.   The harem of Salah Bey is a little lower down;
it is a beautiful old Moorish house, and has been converted into a convent school by the Sisters of the
' Doctrine Chrétienne.'   They have upwards of two

hundred children of the middle class and four hundred of the lower in their ' écoles communales,' besides a large number of boarders.

There is another mosque attached to the *Hanéfi* rite at the corner of the Rue Combes, of which the great beauty is the minaret, which is seventy feet high, of an octagon shape, and with a covered balcony round the top. It is one of the most graceful specimens of the kind possible ; but I tried in vain to get a photograph of it.

We regretted so much not seeing M. Cherbonneau, who is at the head of the French Arabic school here, on the opposite side of the ravine, near the El-Kantra bridge ; but he was gone to Algiers. The college is nearly full ; but we were told that it was a failure as regards the real Arabs, who relapse into their original habits as soon as they return home.

Between the great mosque and the one we have just referred to in the Rue Combes is a famous tomb, built out of Roman remains, and containing the body of a holy marabout from Morocco, whose whole life is said to have been one of devotion and charity. Ascending a few stone steps, you come to a vine-covered terrace, out of which opens the mortuary chamber. By the side of the tomb a venerable-looking old man with a long white beard was praying, and we were told he had been there for thirty years. His face was like that of the pictures of St. Francis of Assisi in ecstasy, and his whole life was spent in fasting and prayer in that sanctuary.

In a court in a narrow street beyond, is a *crèche* kept by the Sisters of Charity for Arab children, which was originally founded by the Maréchale MacMahon, and is now supported by different charitable ladies, each of whom has a small cot or bed of her own. But it is in a miserably damp, unhealthy locality, and so crowded and close that the Sisters' health is seriously injured by it. Their own rooms are the worst of all, as, with their usual charity, they have given up the only airy ones to the children. But we must hope that ere long this invaluable work may be enlarged and extended, and a healthier site found both for the little ones and the community.

Coming home, we stopped at a Beni-Mozabite stall to buy some silver earrings of a kind peculiar to Constantine.

These people form the most curious sect in Algeria. M. Cherbonneau calls them ' Mahometan Protestants.' They go to no mosque or place of worship, and use no forms of prayer. But they are scrupulously honest and truthful in their dealings, and consequently capital traders. They have likewise the monopoly of all the public baths in the three provinces. And this seems to me a good place to give a short account of the religious orders in this country, some knowledge of which is necessary to understand the habits and feelings of the people.

All the Kabyles and Arabs profess the religion of the Prophet, and belong to the rite of Omar and the sect *Méléké* (from the Emir Mélek), which is much the same as that of the *Hanéfi*, of which the Turks are generally members. The only exception to this rule is that of the Beni-Mozabites, of whom I have just spoken, who profess the rite of Ali, but who are looked upon as heretics.

The most important functionaries among them are the marabouts. To them are confided the interests of religion, the preservation of the Mahometan faith in all its integrity, and the enforcing of the precepts of the Koran. Their influence is immense, being both religious and political. Their power is hereditary, and they form, in fact, a species of religious nobility. Their families are rich from the offerings and endowments of the faithful, of which they are allowed the interest ; and they rank higher than the *Chériffs* or *Djouads*, who may be termed the civil and military nobles or chiefs among the tribes, as their sacred character invests them with greater authority. Looked upon as saints, even before their deaths, or at least as men whom constant prayer has united more closely than others to the Divinity, the decisions of the marabouts are considered as final and to be beyond any appeal. They settle public and private quarrels, lay down the law on all questionable points, and often prevent the effusion of blood between different tribes. Or else, with the Koran in one hand and the *flissah,* or pointed sabre, in the other, they preach crusades or religious wars (called El-Djé-had) with the zeal of Peter the Hermit in the Middle Ages.

They generally live in what are called *Zaouyas,* and devote themselves to the instruction of the children and youths entrusted to them by their respective tribes. Some of their disciples assume the title of *Thaleb,* which we should call 'Divinity Students,' and are employed in various subordinate religious offices, as lectors, cate-chists, &c.; or else as care-takers of the *Zaouya* where they reside.

A *Zaouya* signifies either a mausoleum or place of sepulture of the family who has built it; or a place of pilgrimage; or a private mosque, endowed for some particular purpose; or a library, in which different branches of science are taught; or a hospital in which sick travellers are received; but in all cases it implies an inviolable asylum or 'city of refuge,' where men fly from the pursuit of justice or in private feuds, and are safe from vengeance or molestation.

These *Zaouyas* are generally richly endowed, either

N

by deceased benefactors or else by the alms of the faithful. They consist of several houses or suites of apartments, with a mosque in the centre, and a court which serves for the meetings of the Marabouts and discussions on public business. Generally, a *koubba,* such as I have frequently mentioned, is attached to it, containing the body of some revered Marabout, and almost invariably surmounted with a dome or cupola.

But though I have said that the inhabitants of these provinces are almost all of one Mahometan sect, there are, besides, a multitude of religious orders or corporations, bearing the names of their founders, and distinguished by different rites and forms of prayer. Each order attributes its foundation to a dream in which a certain holy Marabout had received directly from the Prophet Mahomet, a revelation of the way (*trik*) in which he is to establish his new order, and the forms of worship which will be most acceptable to God. He is supposed in the same revelation to receive a special mission for this work, which gives him authority to ordain a certain number of disciples or brothers, under the name of Khouans, to whom eternal salvation is assured by a faithful following of the revealed rule.

There are seven of these orders in Algeria, with the names of which I need not trouble my readers. But amongst them are the Khouans Aïssouan, a portion of whose horrible rites I detailed in my chapter on

Algeria ; and their number in Constantine is said to be much greater.

Each of these religious orders is governed by a Khalifa, or Superior-general, who is always nominated beforehand by his predecessor. And this great spiritual authority appoints in each locality a Cheïkh, or Mokaddem, equivalent to an ordinary superior in a religious house, who must himself be a priest, and serve the mosque attached to his *zaouya*. These orders each possess their own *zaouyas* and *koubbas*, into which other Mussulmen are admitted, but without the privilege of reciting the office or rosary with the community, who alone are initiated into the rites peculiar to each order.

Becoming a religious, or being affiliated to a confraternity of this sort, is called : ' Taking the rose of such or such a Marabout' (the word rose being rendered *ouard*).

The Khouans or brothers of the different orders are not obliged to live in Community, although some do so. The greater number return after their profession and live among their respective tribes. Only, in case of a religious war, or at the summons of the Marabout, they must be the first to take up arms ; and are generally the most fanatical of the population. Those that live at home do not adopt any distinctive dress or formula. But when two Arabs meet they will ask one

another : ' To what rose do you belong ? ' ' To that
of Sidi . . . . .' will be the reply ; or else, if he should
belong to no order, he will say simply : ' I wear no
rose, I am only a humble servant of God, to whom I
piously pray.'

The influence of these religious orders or corporations in Algeria is immense. Not to reckon the
Aïssouans, the Derkaouas, and especially the Mouleï-
Tayeb, have a number of their followers in Morocco,
and their father-general resides there. The present
Khalifa of the Mouleï-Tayeb (the most numerous of
these orders) is a direct descendant of the Prophet and
a cousin of the Emperor's. Thus, by their rapid and
mysterious means of communication with each other
through the medium of this brotherhood, the authorities in Morocco possess a lever of action in Algeria
which is always hostile to the French, and forms one of
their great dangers.

This order was established in Morocco about a
century ago ; and its founder on his death-bed pro-
phesied the arrival of the French and their subsequent
overthrow, in terms which have been carefully preserved by the Arabs and handed down by tradition to
their followers.

Addressing his disciples, who were urging the ex-
pulsion of the Turks and the re-establishment of Arab
nationality in the North of Africa, the dying Marabout spoke as follows :—

'Your dominion will extend over the whole of the
Algerian Provinces, and the Turks will be expelled;
but, before the accomplishment of this prophecy, the
country will be conquered and occupied by the *Benou
El-Astor*' (literally, 'the fair, yellow-haired sons of
the north'). 'If you strive to take possession of the
land now, they will ravish your conquest from you.
But be patient; let the northmen drive out the Turks
and take the country first, and *the day will come when
you will, in your turn, overcome them and reign as
lords on the African soil.*'

According to the Arab view of the matter, therefore,
the conquest of Algeria by the French was a matter
of course—had not the Khalifa predicted it? But
the latter half of the prophecy is still unfulfilled, and is
the object of their ardent prayers and aspirations.
All the risings among the tribes, and those continual
revolts, which render the French occupation of the
country from time to time so insecure, are secretly
fomented by these Khouans. At Sétif the other
day, the Marabout of this very sect, sent round the
mysterious summons to the tribes, 'That they were
to rise and arm, *as the hour was come.*' Defeats
and checks do not discourage them; for they only
think that the hour of triumph is deferred owing
to their own sins and want of faith. And the Marabouts are always ready enough to 'improve the occasion' in that sense.

What I have said will prove the nature of the
difficulties which must always surround the French
Government and imperil the safety of their colonists.
The more I heard and talked to different people, the
more I was convinced that it is only by a strong
military occupation that the country can be retained.

But before quitting this subject, I will mention an
anecdote which greatly contributed to the establishment of the power of Abd-El-Kader, and which is
connected with these religious confraternities. Sidi
Abd-El-Kader El-Djelali, the founder of one of
the most ancient orders, was a native of Bagdad,
where no less than seven *koubbas* are erected to his
memory. In 1828, the young Abd-El-Kader and
his father were at Bagdad, and praying in one of these
chapels, when the saint appeared to them and told
them that one of them would some day become Emir
of the Arabs of the West. In 1832, when the province of Oran was in a state of great anarchy and
confusion, a meeting of Marabouts and chiefs was
held in the plain of Egris, in order to choose an Emir
who should re-establish peace and order amongst
them. Various names were suggested, when all of
a sudden a venerable old priest stood up, and said
he had seen the holy founder of his order, El-
Djelali, in a dream, and by his side a gold throne on
which the Marabout had revealed to him that none

was to sit but his descendant, the young Abd-El-Kader, the son of Mahi Eddin. The assembly received the proposal with universal satisfaction; and 300 men on horseback were instantly despatched to demand the young Abd-El-Kader of his father, who had had a similar vision. Their request was granted; and the result was that Abd-El-Kader was unanimously elected Sultan, and received by the Arabs as one sent direct from heaven.

The young Emir always took care to place all his different undertakings and all his new institutions under the patronage of the holy Marabout of Bagdad, from whom he was supposed to receive continual counsels and advice.

Only one of these orders reckons both Arabs and Kabyles among its members, that of *Abd-El-Rhaman ben Kobarin*. This is the only really *national* sect, being founded by a native of Algiers for the purpose of forming a link between those two hostile tribes. Abd-El-Kader caused himself to be enrolled in this order, hoping thereby to bring about a fusion between these races; and then endeavoured to induce the Kabyles to side with him against the French. But he had not reckoned on the interested motives of the Kabyle race, which far outweighed their religious feelings. The Kabyles foresaw greater gain than loss from French occupation, and were likewise strongly averse from leaving their native mountains for a warfare which promised little booty and much risk. So that the Emir found himself defeated in his otherwise far-seeing policy, and had to cope with his Arab forces alone against the French troops—with what success our readers already know.

'MAHOMET'S HAND'

PINS WORN BY ARAB WOMEN.

CHAPTER VII.

BATNA, LAMBESSA, BISKRA, AND OTHER TOWNS IN THE PROVINCE OF CONSTANTINE.

THE moon was shining brightly when we left our comfortable quarters at the Hôtel d'Orient, and scrambled into the coupé of the diligence which was to take us to Batna. This is a journey of twelve hours, and always made at night, which is wearisome enough for those who wish to see the country, though of course, a great saving of time. There is nothing very interesting to be seen on the road till you arrive at some Roman ruins between two great salt lakes, which were covered with wild geese and ducks. To the left is another of those curious mausoleums like the 'Tomb of the Christian,' about which, however, the learned are divided, though it is generally supposed to be the burial-place of Masinissa. This is called the Medrásen, and looks like a series of cylinders diminishing towards the top. But I could only see the outline in the moonlight. At seven o'clock in the morning we reached Batna, a very ugly village with dull streets placed at right angles, an ugly church, a bad inn, and in fact, nothing to recommend it. However, we resolved to stop there for a night or two to see the Cedar Forest which resembles that of Teniet El-Had ; and above all, the Roman remains at Lambessa. Hiring the only carriage in the place, which was a species of little omnibus, we accordingly started directly after breakfast. The road was dreary in the extreme, but we were amply repaid when we first came in sight of the ruins. Pompeii is a town suddenly buried under the ashes which overwhelmed its inhabitants in the midst of their daily occupations ; but Lambessa is a place which seems to have been suddenly abandoned by its population. All its buildings remain standing in the midst of a vast solitary plain, and only the hand of time has worn the edges of its red tufa stones and granite pillars. The first thing which strikes your eye to the left of the old Roman road is a great square pretorium about sixty feet by eighty, of that beautiful rich, reddish-brown tufa of which the tomb of Cecilia Metella is built. A flight of steps with fine columns on each side remains. The interior has been turned into a museum, and contains some beautiful statues, sarcophagi, and marble and alabaster pillars. The outside columns

are composed of three **huge** blocks of circular stones,
without any cement between. **A little** further **on
are two** magnificent **arches,** forming one **of** the forty
gates or triumphal arches which were mentioned **by
the old historians** of Lambessa, and of which fifteen
are still standing. Beyond this gate are the remains
of an aqueduct, of which only four **or** five arches now
exist; **but a** hundred yards to the left are the **ruins**
of the **Temple of Esculapius.** **Four** Ionic columns
resting **on a marble staircase, and** forming part of **the**
façade **of the building, bear an inscription purporting**
that **this temple was built by the orders of Marcus**
Aurelius, and Lucius Virus, and dedicated **to Esculapius and** to Health. **Statues of various gods have**
likewise been discovered **here, and** a Mosaic pavement
on which is the inscription :

BONVS INTRA MELIOR. EXI.

A circus, of which the steps and entrances are well
preserved, stands to the right of this temple. But
all over the vast plain, arches, and gateways, and
beautiful **marble pillars** with delicate capitals, start
out of the grass in various directions. What struck
me most was the excessive solitude of the place. **A
great eagle** poising on **a fallen column of** the preto-
rium was the **only** living thing **to be seen** till we
disturbed a little brown owl perched **on** one of the

beautiful cornices of the temple. At the extreme end of the old town is the tomb of Flavius Maximus, one of the prefects of the third legion. It is a square monument ending in a pyramid, and bears an inscription stating that it was erected by Julius Secundus, centurion of the same legion, in pursuance of the will of Flavius Maximus, who left 12,000 sesterces for its erection. The French have carefully restored this tomb and paid military honours to the ashes of the old Roman, by marching past the monument and firing a salute over it. The modern village is a miserable place, and I pitied the good Sisters of the ' Doctrine Chrétienne' who have set up a school of about fifty children in it, and have not even the consolation of a good priest. Lambessa is a vast penitentiary for ' détenus ' and political prisoners, who are lodged in a large building at the entrance of the village. We were not allowed to go over the prison itself, but we saw some of the prisoners, several of whom were gentlemen, condemned to ten, fifteen, or twenty years' confinement in this miserable place. They eke out a scanty subsistence, in addition to their rations, by their carving, and we bought some of their work. Poor fellows ! they must suffer terribly from both cold and heat, as they have no means of warming the building, and their cells are close under the roof.

Altogether the place left a very painful impression on my mind.

Returning to Batna, I went to the Sisters of the 'Doctrine Chrétienne,' who have a most beautiful school of upwards of 200 children, both boarders and external scholars. Their Superior (the sister of the famous French writer, M. de Maréchale) is a most delightful person, and infuses her large-hearted spirit of charity into the hearts of all with whom she comes in contact. All those who have been trained by her have a peculiar charm of their own, and the whole tone of the house was superior to that of any I had ever seen. Yet she has very delicate health; is always in a state of suffering, and lives in that miserable Batna, without any spiritual or temporal consolations. It made one realise how completely God's grace works in a really holy soul, independently of all outward circumstances. Anyone with less love and less courage would have sunk under the manifold trials and contradictions of her present position. But no ; she said she had always prayed to come and work for souls in Africa, and that now she had her wish, and would never dream of complaining of the difficulties and suffering which attended it.

In the evening I saw the colonel of the garrison, M. Adelher, who has a strong force here, and kindly offered us horses to ride to the Cedar Forest.

But we could not miss the Biskra diligence which only goes twice a week, and was to start the following morning.   At night there was a ' Via Crucis ' Service in the little church, which was thronged with people. The next day was the Feast of the Annunciation, March 25, and fortunately the diligence, which waited for the night mail from Constantine, did not set off till seven, and enabled us to have our service first.   The road was a continual ascent till we reached the karavanserai of Ksour, where we were to change horses and breakfast.   I went out to sketch, and found some curious old Roman ruins, which crop up everywhere in this country, close to which was a picturesque Bedouin encampment ; but the women and children ran away and hid themselves the moment I attempted to take their likenesses.   At Ksour our troubles began.   The road was simply atrocious, and going down an awfully steep pitch with the reckless driving common to these diligence coachmen, our middle wheeler fell heavily on his side, smashing the pole, and very nearly upsetting the great top-heavy machine into the stream.   The poor beast was awfully hurt, but excited no compassion in its brutal driver, who kicked and flogged it till I turned quite sick.   It took a couple of hours to mend the pole, and get the cumbersome diligence out of the slough of despond into which it had sunk.   We walked on till we came to

the karavanserai of the Tamarinds, as it is called, the
road being wild and desolate in the extreme. Here
the diligence at last picked us up, and we came into a
picturesque gorge, leading to El-Kantra, with fine
mountains on both sides, and the river Oued-Kantra
below, which we crossed several times, and always
with difficulty, owing to the steepness of the banks
and the roughness of the stones in the river's bed.
Although we had seven horses, they became thoroughly
exhausted towards the end of the stage ; and in crossing the torrent the last time, before reaching the little
inn of El-Kantra, we found ourselves suddenly thrown
on one side, while the water rushed into the coupé,
the wheel having come off in the middle of the stream.
Scrambling out as best we could, we made our way
to this charming little place, which is situated in the
most beautiful gorge imaginable, between high old
rocks in the centre of an oasis of palms, extending for
several miles. At the bottom of the valley, the Oued-
Kantra rushes in a cascade towards the plain below,
and is spanned by a simple and beautiful Roman arch,
thirty feet in width, over which picturesque bridge the
road passes, connecting the two sides of the defile.
This bridge of El-Kantra, which has given the name
to the oasis, is called by the Arabs *Foum-es-Sahara,*
or the mouth of the Sahara, as it commands the only
approach from the Tell of Algeria to the oriental

Sahara beyond, and its possession is therefore justly looked upon as the key of the whole position. Tired and hot as I was, I could not resist leaving the shade of the little inn to make a sketch of this wonderful pass, through the precipitous rocks of which you perceive not only the palm trees beyond, but strata of almost crimson-coloured salt craigs, which bound the horizon. This place was formerly an important Roman colony, and a variety of Roman inscriptions in marble or bronze are continually being discovered and dug up by the vine-dressers or agriculturists of the oasis. After crossing the bridge, you come to the three villages, or *dacheras*, which are built in the very midst of the palm groves, and surrounded by a high mud wall. Their population amounts to 1,800. The women weave burnouses and coverings for the tents; the men cultivate the palm trees, and have also little crops of cereals, watered by 'sakias' as in Egypt. If the view of the bridge is beautiful, no less lovely is the palm grove from the other side of the gorge, with the magnificent mountains of *Djebel-Gaous* and *Djebel-Essor*, crowning the heights on either side of the pass.

From El-Kantra to El-Outaïa the road crosses a wonderful fossil formation, full of pectens, oysters, cockles, and other sea-shells, though it is difficult to conceive by what convulsion of nature the sea could have arrived at this spot.

At El-Hammam, we again crossed the river close to some thermal springs, which are both hot and salt. To the right is a high conical mountain with strata of marble, gypsum, and salt. The natives call it the Salt Mountain (' Djebel-el-Melah '), and make use of it in a careless sort of way, by picking up the blocks which the winter rains have detached from the rock to sell in the Ziban market. We had plenty of time to study the scenery, as our pole broke again three separate times, having been badly spliced together; so that we did not reach the third stage (of El-Outaïa) till eight o'clock at night, when we ought to have been at Biskra! Here our unhappy vehicle broke down altogether, and we had to remain in the only room of a wretched karavanserai, amidst a quantity of spahis and peasants, for two mortal hours, whilst the diligence was being patched up in various directions. We were so worn out with fatigue that M—— fell fast asleep on one of the wooden settles of the room, and we had to rouse her when at midnight we were told that everything was ready for departure. Once more we scrambled into our coupé and started off in the midst of a furious sand and thunder storm, through which we galloped, with our picturesque escort of spahis; grand flashes of lightning every few minutes illuminating the whole range of the distant mountains and lighting up with an unearthly glow the wreaths of sand which

o

seemed to curl round and envelop our mounted guides
—the whole scene then relapsing into unearthly dark-
ness, while the volume of thunder drowned the noise
of the wheels, and sheer admiration of the grandeur
of the scene overcame not only our fatigue, but the
discomforts of the rough road and the perils of the
river through which we had again continually to ford
before arriving at Biskra, between two and three o'clock
in the morning. Here we discovered that the whole
military population had been very uneasy as to our
safety; for, being six hours behind our time, they
imagined we must have fallen in with hostile tribes
and been robbed by the way. We found most comfortable little rooms at the house of a M. and Madame
Médan, French colonists, who kept a kind of boarding-
house or inn in the little 'Place' behind the market,
and were not sorry to get into clean and comfortable
beds, after being cooped up in a diligence for nineteen
hours! Save at El-Kantra itself, the whole country
from Batna to Biskra is wild and desolate in the
extreme. There are no trees and scarcely any cultivation; but great herds of cattle, camels, and sheep
were feeding at intervals on the mountain-sides,
guarded by small Arab herdsmen. The inhabitants
are a mixture of Arabs and Berbers; being in fact of
those tribes of Biskris or Saharis, whom I have before
mentioned as of Kabyle or Berber origin, but so in-

GROUP OF BISKRA WOMEN.

corporated with the nomad Arabs as to be undis-
tinguishable from them. They live in black camel's
hair tents or mud 'douars,' and their men dress like
the Arabs; but their women have their faces uncovered
like the Kabyles, and are loaded with ear-rings and
ornaments of every kind. A multitude of dogs generally guard the tents, as with the Arabs; but here
they have a rather handsome reddish-brown kind,
being a mixture of the dog and the jackal, instead of
the hideous wolfish-looking hounds we had seen in the
Kabyle villages.

That morning was Sunday, and what was my pleasure on finding my way to the little church to see a
white cornette issuing from a low house just beyond,
as the Angelus bell summoned us to the six o'clock
mass! In spite of their ubiquitous charity, I scarcely
hoped to see the Sisters in the midst of the sandy
deserts and palm groves of the Sahara! I found afterwards that the Superior, Ma Sœur Célestine Angelvy,
was a great friend of the Superior of the Sisters of
Charity in London. They welcomed me most kindly
to their little convent, and insisted upon my having
some delicious chocolate after my long journey, and
then showed me their schools, which are large and
airy, and contained about 200 children. They told
me that they were compelled to close them in summer
for three months, the heat being so intolerable that no

one can stir out till night or very early in the morning.
The Sisters suffer more than other Europeans there ;
as they do not like to adopt the universal custom of
sleeping on their flat roofs—all the more as their house
is overlooked by the large barracks beyond.   But they
owned that to keep in the house was a perfect purga-
tory, and that their beds appeared like burning fiery
furnaces !

After church we went to take a walk in the palm
groves, which are beautiful.   Mr. Dillon's picture in
the exhibition of the Royal Academy last year, of
' Gathering the Date Palms in Egypt,' alone gives an
idea of the beauty of the colouring, the graceful shape
of the palm trees heavy with golden fruit, and the
flickering light and shade thrown by their waving
branches across the richly-irrigated and fertile ground
beneath.   There are upwards of 180,000 palms in this
oasis of the Ziban, or at the rate of 100 trees an acre.
Each palm brings in, from its dates alone, twenty-five
francs a-year to its owner.   The trees begin to bear at
eight or ten years old and go on till they are ninety or
one hundred.   The tax paid to the French Government for each palm is twelve sous a-year, or sixpence
of our money.   The fruit forms in March and is ger-
minated in the following manner.   The male palm
produces a sheaf of blossom, which, when fully open,
is covered with a yellowish white pollen or flour.   The

natives climb up the trees ; carefully cut off this sheaf
and shake the pollen or flour on the newly-formed
dates in the centre or heart of the female tree, and
thus the date is produced. It takes seven months to
arrive at maturity, not being quite ripe till October.
It is only in a very hot sun that the saccharine properties of this fruit are fully developed. The best are
those from Souk, an oasis still further in the desert, as
they do not dry up like the others. Each palm has a
circular space dug round it, containing six cubic feet of
water, which is continually kept full. One tree will,
therefore, require upwards of 300 cubic feet during
the seven months from the incubation till the fruit
arrives at maturity. This system of irrigation is
most carefully attended to, and regular channels from
the river are dug leading to each palm grove, and
never allowed to run dry. The fibres and sheaths of
the palm blossom (which are like the scabbards of a
straight sword) are used for strong ropes and for mix-
ing with mortar or 'doub,' for the native houses. The
fruit is the main food of the population. With the
leaves they make every kind of basket and thatch.
When the tree is past bearing, the head is tapped for
wine (which we tasted but did not like) ; and the tree
is hollowed and used for water-pipes, columns, and
every species of furniture. When used to support the
porticos of houses, these palm logs look almost like old

Roman marble pillars; in fact, both in point of beauty and usefulness no tree equals the palm when seen in these oases, 'with their heads in the fire and their feet in the water,' according to the old Arab saying respecting them. Mr. Hardy, the director of the Botanical Society of Algiers, says that each tree bears seventy-two 'kilos' of dates in the year; and that their value in the market is about equal to that of wheat. He adds that there are seventy different varieties of dates in the Ziban; and that even the hard kernels of the fruit, when softened in water, are given to the cattle, who are very fond of them; so that no portion of this valuable tree is wasted.

After luncheon, our good-natured landlord produced a little carriage of his own and drove us to see the ruins of the old Arab town of Biskra, of which only a minaret and the *kasba* remain. Then he took us to a large botanical garden, planted with bananas, bamboos, and other tropical plants, such as sugar, coffee, rice, &c. But unfortunately the director was absent. We saw also the house of a young French nobleman, who had purchased a large tract of palms in the oasis, and had made a beautiful garden round his château; but he was in France at that moment. I could not help thinking it a very enviable possession, and wondering why a greater number of capitalists did not invest their money in the like manner, if only for the sake of obtaining so desirable a winter residence. The climate for six months in the year is perfectly delicious at Biskra. There is no rain, and the same light, exhilarating air as in Upper Egypt. Between this château and the town is the negro village, inhabited entirely by that race, who live apart from the Arabs in low mud houses, connected by filthy streets, in which multitudes of little naked children, black as ebony, were rolling in the sand. As we came home, the setting sun lit up the range of mountains and the river and desert below with those exquisite roseate tints never seen but in Africa, melting by degrees into purple and green and yellow, in a way impossible to paint but delicious to watch and remember when the dull grey colouring of our own country depresses both body and soul! In the evening the Caïd and his brother came to offer their services, and likewise Colonel Adhemac l'Hey, who commanded the French garrison, and who proposed to lend us horses for a riding expedition on the morrow, which we gladly accepted. We dined at the primitive little *table d'hôte* and were waited upon by the charming children of our host and hostess, who had been educated at Batna, by that admirable Madame de Maréchale whom I have before mentioned, and had learned from her that simple high-bred Christian courtesy which goes so far beyond ordinary politeness. There was a Benediction

service at night after a sermon to the soldiers of the
garrison, who were having a public retreat previous to
the solemnities of Easter.   A painter, M. Dubois, who
lodged, like us, at the Médans, had been spending the
winter at Biskra, and had devoted his talents to painting a beautiful fresco over the chancel representing
our Lord as the Redeemer of the world.   On my way
home I passed by the Arab *cafés*, where women
dressed in gorgeous red and gold stuffs, and covered
with jewels, were dancing to the monotonous sounds of
the tum-tums. The night was as light as day, the moon
throwing sharp shadows from the houses and palm
trees on the bright yellow sand ; and the air felt like
that of a hot July night.   The little rooms of our
house, which was one story high, each opened into a
garden full of sweet peas and other flowers in full
blossom. The heat made it impossible to shut the
doors, and I stayed gazing at the star-bespangled
sky and wondering at the beauty of the whole scene
till I fell asleep.

The ride of the following morning, before the sun rose,
was one of the most delightful expeditions I ever made
in my life. We had capital horses, and cantered along
in and out of the palm groves and quaint villages of
the oasis with their beautiful little minarets, picturesque
bridges made of hollowed palm stems, olive and carouba trees, and magnificent cypresses.   Every turn

seemed more beautiful than the last, and we were
quite unhappy when the increasing heat warned us
that we must return home. I stopped at the Jardin
d'Essai and took a sketch of the town, but was so
mobbed by the women and children of the tents that
it was impossible to go on. They insisted on examin-
ing everything I wore or used ; and one most beautiful
little boy, with glorious black eyes, proceeded to bedaub
himself all over with my paints, till in sheer despair I
gave it up and played with him instead. Camels were
feeding round me with their little ones, and, in spite of
all the stories I had heard of their treachery and bad
temper, it was impossible not to be attracted by their
soft, large, melancholy eyes and to believe that they
were maligned by their detractors.

In the afternoon the Caïd sent us his own carriage,
with a pair of spirited horses and a half mad negro
driver, in which we started at a tremendous pace for
the hot sulphur springs, about ten kilometres from the
town, situated in the midst of arid rocks, with no vegetation whatever, save the rose of Jericho and one or
two similar plants, apparently growing out of the salt
deposited in every direction. On arriving at the spot
we found a square building, in the centre of which was
the boiling spring, and at the side, two or three very
primitive baths were hollowed out of the rock, into
which the water had been conducted by open pipes

and allowed to cool for twenty-four hours before being
used. The properties of these baths are said to be the
same as those of *Hammam-Meskhroutin* of which I
shall give a full account later. But I could obtain no
regular medical information as to the properties of this
Biskra spring. All I could gather from the inhabitants
was that it was invaluable in cases of chronic rheumatism and long-standing affections of the joints; my
landlord told me that he had been entirely crippled for
two or three years in that way, and that a course of
these baths had quite cured him. As I was still suffering from numbness of one leg in consequence of the
rheumatic fever I had had the previous winter, I resolved to try these waters, and was sensibly relieved
by them even after the first experiment. But there is
no proper organisation for invalids in the place, and
not even a towel to be had! So that anyone wishing
to take the necessary course of baths must bring over
everything needful from Biskra. This, however, could
easily be done; and I have very great faith, not only
in the efficacy of the spring itself, but in the effect
of the warm dry climate of this place for all such
ailings. On our way home, we saw a herd of gazelles
feeding, who scampered off, however, long before we
came near them. We reached Biskra safely, which
was rather a marvel, considering the erratic proceed-
ings of our driver, and walked to the kasba, where

we had promised the commandant to come and see the sunset from the bastions. We were a little too soon ; so he good-naturedly took us all over the barracks, and the officers' and men's quarters, and showed us all their live pets, which consisted of gazelles, emus, ostriches, and some handsome dogs. Then we climbed up to the top of the old *kasba* or fort, and there were well repaid by one of those glowing crimson sunsets which Turner alone could have represented, and which flooded the whole country in a sea of light.

One of the most beautiful oases in the Ziban is that of Sidi Okbar, which we decided to visit on the morrow, as it was only twenty kilometres from Biskra. So that at dawn the following morning we started, passed the negro village, and across the river and the sandy plains, on which hundreds of camels were feeding, and then turned to the south-east, where a long dark belt of palms on the horizon pointed to our ultimate destination. To the left was the grand range of the Markadou mountains, tinted a soft yellowish pink by the rising sun ; and at their base were a succession of smaller oases, looking like purple lines in the distance, and only assuming the appearance of palm groves as we came nearer, and could distinguish their graceful shapes. It was nearly noon by the time we reached Sidi Okbar, which is the religious capital of the Ziban, as Biskra is its political centre.

We were received in great state by the Caïd, who gave us coffee in his own house, and then proceeded to show us the mosque and the other lions of the town.　Passing under a dark narrow archway, we came to an exquisitely carved door, supposed to have been executed in the 14th century, and ornamented with most curious hasps and handles in bronze.　This door gives access to the outer court of the mosque, which is the oldest in Algeria.　It is surrounded by a colonnade of twenty-six marble columns, the capitals of which are all different and beautifully carved.　The minaret is very graceful, and smaller above than below; and the view from thence is very extensive. The interior of the mosque is richly coloured, especially the nimbar and mihrab.　To the right is the tomb of the emir and saint Sidi Okbar, who was surprised and murdered by a Kabyle chief, who had been his prisoner, and whom he had wantonly insulted.　But charity or humanity are not reckoned among Mussulmen qualifications for canonisation. None but the faithful are allowed to enter the enclosure where rests the sacred body.　We were only allowed to peep through some beautiful pierced stone windows, carved in a peculiar manner, alternately cross and lozenge-shaped, and saw a small mortuary chapel, the walls of which were decorated with paintings, after the manner of exvotos, with a coffin in the middle, covered

with rich green silk hangings, beautifully embroidered,
and with the usual banners and ostrich eggs suspended
above. Let in to one of the pillars which support
the chapel is an Arabic inscription recording the name
and title of the deceased, with the addition of the
words : ' On whom may God have mercy.' This
inscription, which is in Cufic characters, dates from
the first era of the Hegira, and is supposed to be
the most ancient in Algeria. The tomb itself is a
great place of pilgrimage, as may be seen by the
innumerable Arab names engraven or written on
the walls. A little cupboard let into the wall contains
some curious old MSS. and books, but we were not
allowed to look at them. After leaving the mosque
we walked through the principal streets, and to the
market, where we bought some curious little circular
looking-glasses, covered with leather, which the Biskri
women fasten to their waists with red leather strips,
and also some beautiful purplish red stuff, striped with
white, to make petticoats. Then the Caïd took us to
see the making of the haïks and gandouras, which
were beautifully fine. One woman especially was
working at a large loom by herself, and introducing
every kind of variety into the soft texture she was
weaving. Then we returned to the Caïd's to dinner,
a quantity of various dishes being put before us,
ending, as usual, with cous-cous, which this time

was very good. The intense heat made the rest and
shade very acceptable; and our host made a fearful
effort and sacrifice (we were afterwards told), by
dining with us himself, which he had never before
done with any woman. After dinner a mysterious
communication was made with our guide, which resulted in our being taken into a garden, full of orange
trees, and shaded by large palms, in which we were
introduced to the Caïd's wife, a young lady of twenty,
of whom he was evidently very proud. She had
regular, straight features, and dark eyes, but looked
very melancholy, and seemed afraid to stir or speak.
She was dressed in a gorgeous red dress, spangled
with gold stars, with a green sash, and a soft white
and violet gauze scarf thrown over her head, and was
literally covered with jewels. Round her neck, arms,
ankles, and head were rows upon rows of gold, pearls,
emeralds, and other precious stones, while ' Mahomet's
hand' confined both sides of her haïk. She sat on
a little stool perfectly immovable, while I took her
likeness and that of her waiting-maid, which delighted
the Caïd, who proudly wrote her name and his own
underneath the sketch in Arabic characters. From
the garden we had a lovely view of the graceful
minaret of the mosque, with its lancet windows; while
across it, a magnificent palm appeared to be thrown
which shaded a fountain, where some little calves were

drinking. But no shade of satisfaction crossed the face of the lady when we admired her beautiful garden. She only looked frightened and bored, so that at last we took our leave and saw her disappear hastily and joyfully by a covered way into her (harem) prison; while we thanked our kind and courteous host, and getting into our little carriage drove back to Biskra. What is most remarkable in the first look of this village of Sidi Okbar is the quantity of palms, which so completely overshadow the houses, that, at a distance, nothing but their feathery branches is visible.

Our next expedition was to a very picturesque village about five miles from Biskra in the opposite direction, called Sidi Becker. A magnificent sycamore fig-tree shaded the river, over which a bridge of hollowed palm logs was thrown. The minaret is beautiful, and in the centre of the court is a large group of palms and a picturesque fountain, round which were grouped a number of women and children, covered with silver ornaments and charms. There is a thickness of feature about the women which prevents their being really handsome, in spite of their dark eyes and straight noses. On my return I amused myself by drawing a girl of eighteen, who persistently stared in at my bedroom window till I revenged myself by sketching her, though she ran away the moment she discovered my occupation.

In the evening we were invited to the Caïd's house, and introduced to his wife and daughter, who are both very handsome. The mother sat in an alcove, gorgeously dressed; and by her side were two very pretty grandchildren, one of whom was fast asleep on a little bed, and the other stared at the apparition of the two strange European women as if he never would recover from his astonishment. The daughter was a widow and very sad. It appeared that her marriage had really been one of inclination, and that she was inconsolable at her husband's death. She was not in black, but wore no ornaments, which, with them, is a sign of mourning. Our conversation was carried on by the second son, who was one of the handsomest Arabs I ever saw, and spoke very tolerable French. He expressed the most ardent wish to visit England, which his brother had done at the time of the Exhibition in 1862, and was evidently very much dissatisfied with his present position at home. The old lady had had nine children (as she told us), all as fine grown and good looking as this one, of whom she was evidently very proud. They gave us delicious coffee in the Arab fashion, and Souk dates; and seemed very much amused at our appearance. M——'s hat especially attracted their attention, and still more her immense quantity of hair. We walked home by the most glorious moonlight possible, the houses and palms looking as if they had been cut out of the dark blue night sky, the shadows being sharper and darker than in noonday. Biskra is certainly the most delicious climate in the world during the winter and spring seasons; and living is so cheap that I cannot understand why more people do not go there whose health compels them to strive to escape English damp and fogs. Our whole bill at Mde. Médan's, including a little carriage, was only 100 francs; and for that we had had excellent breakfasts, luncheons, and dinners for M—— and myself and three servants, and most comfortable, clean beds and rooms. The diligence fares from Batna to Biskra were twenty-three francs each; from Batna to Constantine only fourteen; so that the journey is as inexpensive as all the rest.

The following morning, to our great sorrow, we left Biskra in spite of the entreaties and remonstrances of the Commandant, who considered that our going at that moment involved the greatest possible risk. He told us that he had certain information of the rising of the Arabs; that all the farms on the road-side had been burnt and destroyed, and that it would be much safer to come into the Citadel with the Sisters of Charity, who had already taken refuge there, and wait for quieter times. It is very fortunate that we were not

infected by his fears, as that happened to be almost
the last week when the journey could be accomplished
in safety. Seeing that we were bent on departure,
he determined to send us an escort of six Spahis,
who were very ornamental, but I doubt if they would
have been of any use had we met with any hostile
tribes. One of the said Spahis had the most villanous
countenance I ever beheld, and his cruelty to his
horse, in which he was continually digging his fearfully
long Arab spurs (which cut like a knife, and had
besides a great pointed spike in the centre), completed
my disgust. Seeing that his horse was covered with
blood, we insisted on his dismounting and giving us
the spurs, which only a threat of reporting him to the
authorities induced him at last to do. I am afraid
that the tales of our childhood as to the Arab's treatment of his horse and his affection for it, are entirely
fabulous. I never saw so much cruelty to animals as
among the Arabs generally ; and when once I indignantly made one of them understand that in England
he would be put in prison for his brutality, as there
was a law for the prevention of cruelty to animals in our
country, he only laughingly remarked, ' that if it were
in force in Africa, the whole nation would be in prison
at once!' I can honestly say that it was the only
thing which spoiled my pleasure in Algeria ; for it is
almost worse to see cruelty exercised towards brutes

than men, for they, at any rate, can complain of their wrongs.

To return to our journey. When we arrived near El-Outaïa, we found the road almost blocked up with Arabs and camels, gesticulating and screaming as usual. They too had been alarmed at the prospect of hostilities, and were moving their flocks to safer camping-grounds. At El-Outaïa itself, the owners of the karavanserai were weeping with fright. '*Fifteen thousand* Arabs were only four kilometres off; and they would all be massacred before morning unless they escaped at once.' To our request for breakfast, they turned a deaf ear: 'Les Arabes! Les Arabes!' was all the reply; and as 'there is only a step from the sublime to the ridiculous,' so in the midst of my very sincere sympathy for these poor people, who were on the eve of losing their little all, I could not help laughing at the old mother, who, flinging her apron over her head, exclaimed: 'O! mon cochon; mon *cher* cochon!' In vain we advised them to be calm and quiet, and stay where they were, at least for a time. They would not listen to us, and only exclaimed at our madness in persisting to go on to El-Kantra, as they declared we should come upon the hostile tribes within half an hour after leaving the karavanserai; that they had burnt Mr. S——'s farm and were in full march on El-Outaïa. We promised to send back a Spahi to warn them,

should we perceive the enemy's scouts on the hills, and
then persevered in our journey, and saw . . . .
nothing whatever! Not an Arab was to be seen till
we got near El-Kantra itself, nor a single tent, or
horseman; only some tiny Arab boys were herd-
ing their cattle on the plains, and ran away and hid
themselves as we drove by. I have always thought
that the absurd panics of the French about the Arabs
often create the very evils they dread. And I do not
believe that even in the late serious rising there was
any mischief done except at some farms near Lambessa; so that the colonel of the little Biskra garrison
might have slept calmly in his bed.

We slept at El-Kantra this time, at the not very
comfortable little inn ; but I wanted to have more time
to draw, and explore that wonderfully beautiful gorge.
The next morning we again took the diligence to
Batna, and were received with open arms by dear
Madame de Maréchale, who had an excellent dinner
ready for us on our arrival. I called on Colonel
Adelher to tell him of the panic at Biskra and to beg
of him, in the name of the Médans and other Europeans there, to send some more troops to reinforce the
garrison ; which he promised to do. And then, returning once more to our coupé, we arrived, after a
somewhat tedious night journey, at Constantine.

We spent the remaining two days in visiting our old

haunts and taking leave of the many kind friends we had made there; but we found a terrible change of climate—from the Indian heat of Biskra to positive snow! Constantine is very cold in winter, from the height of its position and the vicinity of snowy mountains; and it is well that invalids should be prepared with warm clothes for this place on their way to and from the sunny desert.

At four o'clock the following morning we reluctantly wished 'good-bye' to Constantine and started in the diligence for Guelma. The last thing we saw in the early dawn, as we sadly crossed the beautiful bridge which spans the ravine, was an old Numidian stork slowly wending its way from the minaret top to the gorge below.

The road to Guelma is almost impassable for carriages and a terrible strain on the horses; the new metalled road is not yet completed, and when we reached a karavanserai called Le Kroubs, our driver simply struck across country, fording rivers and breaking down hedges in a sort of steeple-chase fashion, which would have been very alarming to nervous passengers. We preferred walking the greater part of one stage and gathering some of the beautiful flowers which grew in the meadows, including white narcissus, tulips, and crocuses. Till we neared Guelma, the road was very dreary and flat; but then the scenery becomes more like that of Milianah, with fine woods and mountains beyond.

Guelma is an uninteresting little French town built on the ruins of the ancient Calama, of which a fortress and ramparts alone remain. There is a tidy little museum in an old circular temple containing some interesting statues, marble pillars, and inscriptions discovered during the construction of the modern town. The inn here was the only bad and dirty one we had found in Algeria, and we were not tempted to prolong our sojourn beyond the following morning, when, being Palm Sunday, we stayed to go to church and get our palms at the pretty little church of St. Augustine, which stands in the principal 'Place.' There were very large schools as usual of the sisters of the 'Doctrine Chrétienne,' and the children had the unusual custom of decorating their palms with cakes and sugar-plums, which I did not admire. A little beyond Guelma lies Souk Harras, the ancient Tagaste and the home of St. Monica, where St. Augustine was born on November 13, 334; Patricius, his father, being prefect of the town.

After church, we joyfully left our dirty quarters and started in a little carriage for Hammam-Meskhroutin or the 'accursed baths,' to visit which had been one of the main objects of our journey to the province of Constantine. The road winds past a large farm belonging to an enterprising French colonist, M. Vigier, and then, turning sharply round to the left, ascends a narrow and picturesque valley with the river Seïbouse below and a fine range of mountains above, till you reach the high plateau on which the hot springs first come in sight—or rather a soft white cloud of sulphurous smoke. We drove straight to the house of Mr. Lambert's housekeeper, who had prepared a little cottage for us, one story high, with three bright, clean, little rooms, according to the instructions sent her by Mr. Lambert (then governor of Algeria), on whose property these baths were situated. There is no hotel; but an embryo kŭrhaŭs, a military hospital, and a set of little baths, in separate houses, built just above the springs. But how describe this most curious place? A succession of white cones remain, where the issues of the spring have changed their course; and in the centre is a group of separate pillars of stone, which gave rise to the following Arab legend. A rich Arab, determining to contract a marriage with a very beautiful girl within the forbidden degrees, and in spite of Mussulman law, gave a magnificent feast on the occasion; when, just before the conclusion of the wedding ceremony, a tremendous earthquake supervened—the demons were let loose, and all the unfortunate bridal party were turned into stone—including the father and mother of the bride and the Caïd, who had presided at the ceremony! They even point to the granulated fragments of sulphur below as being petrified 'cous-cous,' the remains of the marriage feast. The water is creamy white, like milk, and issues in boiling springs from every part of the ground. These unite in a beautiful cascade, which falls over a sheet of rocks of glittering whiteness (shaded with exquisite pink, green, and orange) into the torrent below. The waters of these springs are hotter than any other known, save the Geysers in Iceland and those of Las Trincheras in South America. The temperature of the Geysers is 109°; that of Las Trincheras 96· 6°, while that of Hammam-Meskhroutin is 95°. Their pro-perties are much the same as those of Bagnères, Aix en Savoie, and Eaux Bonnes, being composed of chlorate of soda, sulphur, and sulphate of lime in certain pro-portions. They are excellent for every description of rheumatism, neuralgia, glandular affections, sciatica, and the like; and the water is administered in douches and by inhalation as well as in ordinary baths. It is altogether a most singular spot, and by moonlight the scene of the Arab ghost story is most weird and beau-tiful. Thick clouds of steam rise out of the earth in every direction, occasionally displaying, and then shrouding altogether, these spectral pillars, giving to the whole scene an appearance of reality which is absolutely startling. The finest view of the Geysers, however, is

from below; the boiling streams flowing in a cataract
down a sheer whitish, pinkish yellow rock (as I have
said before) to the depth of some 200 feet, amidst a
cloud of steam on which the sun, when shining, throws
the most exquisite prismatic colours. I tried in vain to
paint it; the effects varied every moment. Large olive
and acacia trees shaded the bottom of the dell; and in
the stream below the Arabs were washing their clothes,
and boiling their eggs and vegetables. Fine mountains back the glen; but they attract a good deal of
rain and cold to this place, where the season does
not begin till May or June, and ends in October.
Beyond the kürhaüs is a beautiful and picturesque
glen, full of red stalactites and grottoes; and above
and below there are delicious walks through woods of
olives and lentisk, while oleanders and a multitude of
wild flowers fringe the little streams. These baths
were well known to the Romans, and Mrs. Lambert's
brother took us about a couple of miles off to see the
old Roman cisterns which still exist, and where there
are a fresh set of springs; but these are ferruginous, and
start out of the rocks on the right bank of the Oued-
Chedakhra. These waters contain a mixture of iron
and sulphur, and are almost identical with those of Spa
and Pyrmont. The efficacy and value of such ferruginous springs alongside of the others are well known to
the profession. We gathered a quantity of petrified

leaves and sticks, looking like the whitest coral, from the
brink of these Roman baths.   The path to them winds
through a wood, famous for its panthers and wild cats ;
but we did not see any.   Only two beautiful eagles
soared down from the mountains above and perched for
a few minutes on a rock near where we were resting.   It
is a pity that no good arrangements have yet been made
for the accommodation of the bathers, who are de-
pendent for their food on the proprietor of the springs;
unless, as in our case, furnished with letters from the
governor.   But perhaps things are better managed
when the regular season begins.

In the evening we strolled again to the cascade and
were more and more amazed at the beauty and strange-
ness of the scene, and the quantity of water thrown up
at one time.   Two of the springs alone produce 84,000
litres an hour, and their number is continually increasing.[1]   The temperature of the water is such that,
wishing to get some to wash our hands, we had to
wait a full hour before it would cool sufficiently to
use.   One curious effect of the exhausted cones is,
that the earth having accumulated above and the
birds having dropped seeds on it, they appear like a
species of gigantic flower-pots, from which graceful

---

[1] Plombières produces only 10,416 litres an hour.

Barèges	„	7,500	„
St. Saviour's	„	6,000	„
Bourbonne	„	5,000	„

ferns and grasses fall on the sides of the cones. In the night we were woke by the shock of an earthquake, which upset everything in the room. It always appeared to me as if a very little would be required to precipitate all the inhabitants of this spot into the boiling cauldron below! The crust of earth, or rather sulphur, on which you walk, is so thin, that it is even difficult to escape being scalded without proper precautions, by the little streams which perpetually cross your path; and hence the Arabs have invented a multitude of stories connected with the wedding legend, and no power on earth would induce them to go near this, which they consider 'accursed,' spot after dark. To sum up what I have said for the benefit of invalids, it appears to me that nothing could be better for persons who cannot afford the expensive watering-places of the south of Europe, than to seek the baths of Hammam-Meskhroutin. We were there before the season began, but we were told that there was an excellent doctor at the head of the establishment; and every day the arrangements for the comfort of the patients are improving. Last year upwards of 200 came; who were more or less benefited and some quite cured. The expense of the passage from Marseilles to Bona is 118 francs first class, and 95 francs second class. The diligence fare from Bona to Guelma is only eight francs, and from thence a little carriage or the omnibus takes you to the baths, which are about an hour and a half's drive from Guelma. Therefore, reckoning the whole expense from Paris, the cost would be as follows :—

	First Class.	Second Class.
From Paris to Marseilles . .	. frs. 96	. frs. 72
From Marseilles to Bona . .	. 118	. 95
From Bona to Guelma . . .	. 8	. 8
Omnibus	. 3	. 3
	225	178

The expense of the journey, which a 10*l.* note would cover, would be more than compensated by the excessive cheapness of living and lodging.

Returning to Guelma we went to see the Arab market, which was crowded and held close to the old theatre ; and then started by diligence for Bona. The only thing we regretted at Guelma was a little pet wild boar, mahogany coloured, and striped with black, which drank milk out of the spout of a teapot, and considered himself quite as one of the family.

The road to Bona is very picturesque, winding up to the top of a very high hill, from whence there was really a magnificent view of the mountains and the plain below, with the river Seïbouse running through it, and the lake Fetzara to the left, famous for its wild fowl. As we descended towards the sea-shore, we passed through smiling gardens and orchards, and carefully cultivated ground—a rare sight in Algeria. Bona itself is a bright little town, situated on the sea-shore, in the centre of a bay, which is protected by two

spits of land projecting into the sea (each crowned by
an old fort), from the violence of the gales to which this
coast is subject. The modern French town is like a
small Marseilles, with a fine background of mountains.
Part of the old town remains intact; including the
picturesque *kasba*, now turned into a barrack, to
which the ascent is by a well engineered road, bordered
by trees, aloes and gardens, reminding me of the way
to the Pincio from the Piazza del Popolo. There is a
picturesque square or 'place,' planted with trees, in
the centre of which is a garden, and a white marble
fountain, while the shops round it on three sides are
arcaded; on the fourth is the fine old mosque of Djama-
El-Bey. On the top of the minaret were my favourite
storks, which abounded in Bona. We went afterwards
to a photographer's, and on mounting up to his
'atelier,' which was very near the sky, we found a
female bird sitting, and were told that her nest had
been the scene of a singular battle the day before.
The male had brought a serpent to his mate, which
somehow or other slipped away. There was a great
hunt, but the news of the treasure got wind among the
other storks, and when the reptile at last turned up
in the eave of the roof, there was a battle royal for
its possession, during which the serpent was literally
cut into a thousand pieces. The only annoyance, in
fact, caused by these birds (which are looked upon, as

in Germany, as quite the friends of the family) is their
habit of bringing these snakes into the houses. For
they often get away and lay their eggs, which are
quite soft, under the tiles or in the rooms, and are
sometimes of a very dangerous kind. When the
storks return to their nests, they bow gravely to each
other and snap their bills together, making a peculiar
sharp noise, which the Arabs say is their thanksgiving
to God for a safe return. In the Moslem tombs, a
little trench is often dug to catch the rain-water for
the storks, with the idea that even after death these
birds shall find refreshment at their hands.

But while talking of the storks, I am forgetting St.
Augustine, who is the principal interest of Bona.
My first visit had been to the cathedral, which is a
very handsome Byzantine building, dedicated to St.
Augustine, in the Place Napoleon. It contains some
good frescos of the life of the saint, and of St. Monica,
and some valuable relics. But my chief object was
to see Hippone, the ancient Ubbo, which is about
two miles from Bona, and which was the home of
St. Augustine and the seat of his bishopric. Here he
was ordained priest in 390, and afterwards coadjutor
to Valerius, whom he succeeded in that see in 395.
Here too, in 397, his 'Confessions' were written ; while,
from 413 to 426, he was occupied in his famous work
the 'City of God.' Hippone had the happiness of

possessing St. Augustine for thirty-five years, and they
were the years of its glory and renown, for Carthage
was then a town of only secondary importance. The
year after St. Augustine's death, that is, in the month
of August 431, Hippone was taken by the Vandals.
The inhabitants had defended themselves valiantly
for two months, but their resistance only served to
exasperate the conquerors, and when the city at last
fell, it was very nearly burnt to the ground. The
only thing which escaped was the cathedral and palace
of St. Augustine, and by a special providence, his
library and valuable MSS. which he had left by will
to his church, escaped the action of the flames. Re-
taken in 534 by Belisarius, Hippone was restored to a
portion of its former splendour, but fell into the hands
of the Arabs in 697, who completed the ruin the
Vandals had begun. The space occupied by the old
walls is about sixty acres. All that is left at present
are the Roman cisterns, a portion of the aqueduct,
and the walls of the bishop's palace. On one side of
the ruins a little chapel has been erected, where a
good old priest, lately dead, used to offer daily the
Holy Sacrifice. He had a little cottage close by, and
his greatest wish was to induce some fathers of the
Augustinian order to settle there, and have a mission
on that spot. Beautiful acanthus leaves grew everywhere among the ruins, which were shaded by old

olive trees, and covered with clematis, dog-roses and
wild flowers. The kind Superior of the sisters of the
' Doctrine Chrétienne' (the Mère Céline) had gone
with me ; and together we clambered up the steep path
leading to an olive wood, in the centre of which is a
large circular white marble monument to St. Augustine, with a bronze statue of the saint above. Here,
on his feast, mass is said, litanies are sung, and a
processional service follows. The view from this
spot is quite magnificent, overlooking Bona and the
blue Mediterranean to the left, and Mount Edough to
the right. We could not help thinking how often
St. Augustine must have looked upon that self-same
scene, for nature is unchangeable. Coming down
the hill we went to visit a large orphanage a little
beyond Hippone, kept by the same sisters of the
' Doctrine Chrétienne ;' who have upwards of 200
orphans there, and one of the most beautiful houses,
farms, and gardens I ever saw. The children cultivate the whole, and are taught every kind of industrial work. In the evening, the Superior showed me
their house in the town, which is very large. They
have twenty-seven sisters and literally *hundreds* of
children of all races and ages, divided in a multitude
of different class-rooms. Some are boarders, but the
greater number are only external scholars. These
ladies have also the care of the civil hospital, where

twelve sisters are employed. The children have beautiful voices, and some of the elder ones sang me a
'cantique' to St. Augustine, in parts, which was one
of the prettiest things I ever heard.

The next morning the consul and the mayor came
to bring us tickets for the government railroad to
Mokta-El-Hadid, the great iron mine about six
leagues from Bona. The line passed through a
beautiful and richly cultivated valley, running between
two ranges of hills, till we came to the great lake of
Fetzara, of which we had had a bird's-eye view on
our way from Guelma. Here our only fellow-passengers, who were sportsmen, left the train to go and
shoot wild ducks, we promising to pick them up on
our return. About an hour further on, we reached
the iron mine, where we were courteously received by
the director of the works, who proceeded to explain
everything to us. Its great peculiarity consists in
the ore being picked out from the rocks above, and
not under ground. There seems none below a certain
level. This ore is sent straight to France to be
smelted, as they cannot work it on the spot for want
of coal—the only undiscovered treasure in Algeria.
The men work by task-work, and earn from three to
five francs a day. The ore is thrown into little carts,
which run on a tramway connected with the railway,
which conveys it straight to the port at Bona, so there

is little or no transhipment. The director told us that
his men suffered a good deal from fever in the summer
owing to the vicinity of the lake; but that, in consequence
of the war, he was very short of hands, as the Arabs
would not work steadily. The ore is superior to any
found in France, especially for cannon, and will
consequently increase in value year by year. I
sketched the Lake Fetzara, which is ten or twelve
leagues long, with the range of fine mountains above,
of which Mt. Edough is the principal. But Mokta-
El-Hadid itself offers no point of interest, and we
were rather glad when the train started to return to
Bona. Nothing could equal the kindness of the
mayor here, who placed his horses and carriage at
our disposal during the whole time of our visit, which
was the more acceptable as none were to be hired in
the town.

The following day we drove to the old Genoese
fort at the Cap de Garde, passing through the Kasba
gate by the botanical gardens, in which every species
of tropical plant is cultivated. The road runs along
the sea shore, and is rather like a bit of the Corniche,
with the blue Mediterranean on one side, and mountains and ravines and wooded gorges on the other.
Only, instead of the terraced gardens and rich cultivation of Savoy, nothing but the dwarf fan-palms grew,
interspersed with wild lavender, yellow broom, white

and purple cistus, wild thyme, and other flowering shrubs, scenting the whole air. I have not mentioned the exquisite olive-green shade of the younger branches of the fan palm, which gives such a beautiful variety of tint, where, otherwise, the colouring would be too monotonous. At every turn of the road we came upon charming little fine sandy bays, covered with shells, where it was almost impossible not to stop and pick them up. Between the Cape and the old Genoese fort are a number of very curious grottos looking towards the sea. The first seemed cut out of the rock, and served as a shelter for some flocks of goats and their keepers. The two others, called the Grottos of the Saints, are hollowed out in every kind of fantastic shape, and are supposed to have been the hiding-places of the Christians during the Vandal persecution. A little further on is a large marble quarry, worked by the Romans, who drew from thence the material for most of the monuments at Hippone. In the interstices and fissures of the marble grow the carouba, vine, nopal and fig trees with great luxuriance, and just beyond, is the Cap de Garde, with its beautiful lighthouse, perched on the top of a mass of rocks, which may be seen at a distance of ten leagues. This was our last expedition in Algeria, as the following morning we were to start in the steamer for Tunis; but, before concluding this description of the country and its inhabitants, I will devote a short chapter to the history of its present administrative policy; a question which the recent march of events has made one of great interest, especially to all lovers of France and the French people.

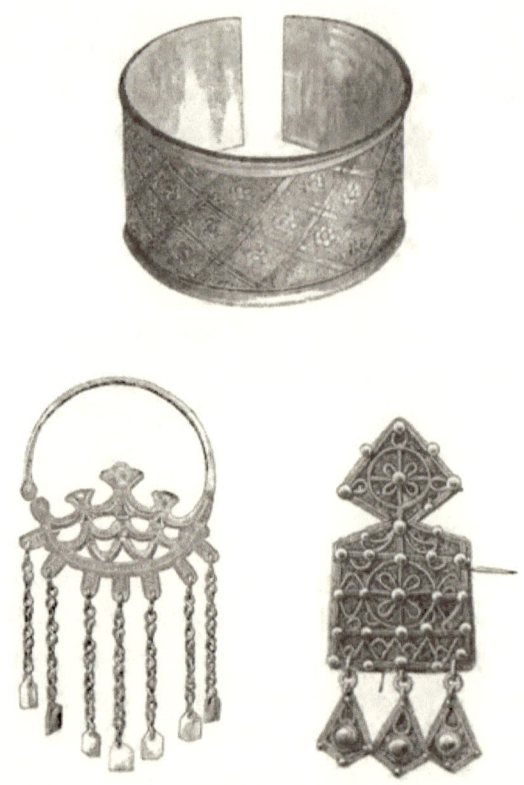

LEGLET, BROOCH, AND EAR-RING.

CHAPTER VIII.

ON THE FRENCH GOVERNMENT IN ALGERIA.

ONE of the greatest difficulties which the French have had to cope with in Algeria, has been not the conquest of the country, but its subsequent organisation.

Their government of the native races has been based on the policy of Abd-El-Kader. The Emir had divided the power between the Khalifas, the Aghas, and the Kaïds; who, in time of war, acted as generals, but in time of peace were entrusted with all legal and political functions, and were likewise charged with the levying of taxes, and the administration of the finances. A functionary called *L'Oukil-el-Soltan* had the superintendence of the crown lands and of the farmers who worked them. The Kadi, chosen among the Thaleb (or wise men), was charged with all acts pertaining to the civil law, such as marriages, divorces, guardianships, successions, sales, &c.; so that in cases of dispute or litigation it rested with him to give the final decision, award damages, and the like.

This simple form of government rested on three
great principles : *religion, fear,* and *interest.* Its advantages consisted, not only in its simplicity but in
its strength ; and above all, in the promptness and
rapidity of its execution.   The decisions of the magis-
trates rested principally on the laws contained in the
Koran, which are very minute ; and also on the rules
and customs laid down by their legal authorities in
certain cases ; just as with us, decisions are given in
pursuance of certain precedents, and so 'ruled' by
such and such a judge.

But the government of the Emir was, above all,
a despotism. His own prestige, and the necessities
of the war, had enabled him to mould the Arabs to
an almost blind obedience. In addition to the ordinary taxes sanctioned by the Koran, he continually
came upon his people for supplementary contributions
under the name of *el-maoûna,* which signifies 'extraordinary supplies.'   In the division of the tribes
into khalifats or provinces, however, he did not sufficiently take into account either the sympathies of the
people or their natural frontiers ; and in some cases
(such as the Medjehers and the Bordjias), the whole
tribe were suddenly transplanted from their native
soil to other spots, where the Emir considered they
would be less exposed to the seductions or wiles of his
enemies.   These arbitrary measures and the multi-

plication of taxes made him, at last, unpopular among the Arabs, and contributed a good deal to the ultimate success of the French.

This was the state of things in Algeria till the fall of Abd-El-Kader in 1847, which resulted in the submission of the whole of the 'Sahel' and 'Tell,' although it was not till 1857 that the Kabyle country and part of the Sahara yielded to the French forces. The names of Cavaignac, Changarnier, Canrobert, Pelissier, Yussuf, and last, not least, Mac Mahon, are too well known in connection with this protracted struggle to need mention here. But then came the question of reconstruction. The French began by dividing the conquered country into three provinces, under one governor-general; and these three provinces into military and civil departments, each of which was subdivided into a certain number of circles, according to its extent and importance. These circles were commanded by staff-officers, corresponding directly with the war minister and the governor-general. So far all was easy; but then came the grouping of the tribes. A tribe, which is the natural extension of a family, forms the patriarchal existence of an Arab. The number of persons in each tribe varies considerably, according to the character of the chief, the consideration in which he is held, the size of his family, and the number of the tents who have come to put themselves under his protection and to promise him obedience. The chief's tent (*bit*) is in all cases the centre of authority, while the circle of tents (called *douar*) is confided to a sheik, who is a species of mayor. The whole tribe is commanded by a kaïd; several of these tribes joined together form an aghalik, and several aghaliks, a khalifat.

The French Government resolved to respect the existing state of things, only reserving to itself the right of a voice in the election of the kaïds, who were to be responsible for the submission of their respective tribes. On the day of their investiture, they each receive from the French a burnous and the seal of office; but have to present a horse fit for cavalry service, in token of vassalage, instead of the sum of money which was formerly exacted by the Emir. Besides the kaïd, there are three other authorities among the Arabs deserving mention; the khalifa, a native chief in the pay of France; the agha, who holds a military employment directly under the staff officer in command of the 'circle'; and the kadi, who is chosen among the thalebs, or wise men, and officiates as the religious guardian of the orphans or minors among the tribes. All these different function-aries were placed by the French Government under the supervision of what is called the 'Bureau Arabe,' which has been often alluded to, and is established

at all the strategical points in the country. The head
of this important office is the only intermediate agent
between the Arabs and the French Government. He
must be perfectly conversant not only with the Arabic
or Kabyle dialects of the district in which he is placed,
but he must become intimately acquainted with their
manners and customs, their religious usages, and in
fact with every peculiarity belonging to each tribe.
His business is to watch the conduct of the kaïds and
other Arab officials ; to win their confidence, if possible,
or if not, to give instant notice of any hostile intentions on their part against the government, or of any
conspiracy which may be brewing amongst them
against French interests. He is called upon to decide
in all quarrels between the French and the natives ;
and he should make it his business constantly to visit
the different tribes, and become the protector of the
oppressed, and the redresser of all wrongs and injustices. On him, also, rests the equalising of the
burdens of taxation. He is bound to keep a register
at his office of all occupiers or holders of land and of
the amount of produce of each holding, whether in
cattle, grain, or from other sources ; so that from
thence correct statistical information may always be
obtained. In addition to these grave responsibilities,
he is charged with the payment of the Spahis,
Makhzen, Askars, and other irregular cavalry, a

certain number of whom are always at his disposal
for active service when required.   All the minor
'Bureaux Arabes' are centralised in the chief town in
each province, that is, in Constantine, Oran, and
Algiers.   And they again are obliged to report themselves to the head 'Bureau' of all, which is attached
to the staff of the governor-general of Algeria.

Now nothing can be more perfect and beautiful
in theory than this establishment.   By its means all
the tribes are kept under constant supervision, and
their peculiar needs and wishes become intimately
and accurately known to their European rulers.   But,
unfortunately, the persons employed in this delicate
and responsible office have not always been worthy
of the high trust reposed in them.   In many cases
grave injustices and great peculations have been the
result of such unlimited powers ; so that when I was in
Algeria, immense discontent was felt and expressed
among the natives against the whole system, and
serious discussions arose among men in office as to
the policy of abandoning it altogether.   In what way
adequately to replace the existing organisation will
be a problem of immense difficulty.   There must be
some intermediate agent between the two races : and
neither the prefects who are charged with the civil
administration, nor the general officers on whom rests
the superintendence of the military, can possibly

perform, unaided, such arduous and peculiar functions.

As to the finances of the country, they will always
be a difficulty until capitalists can be found who will
bring money into the colony and develope its enormous resources. The Arab taxes consist mainly of
what are called the *aachouar*, or the tenth of the crops
(valued either by the quantity sown, or the look of the
standing corn), and the *zikkat*, or a tax on property and
cattle at the rate of five per cent. It was, however,
found impossible to collect these taxes in the mountainous districts or on the frontier, so that the French
Government compromised the matter by a species of
tribute called *lezmà*. The responsibility of the different tribes in this matter is very fairly recognised.
Again, if some flagrant wrong has been committed in
a certain district—say the burning of a wood, or of a
homestead (the commonest form of Arab aggression)—
all the *douars* or encampments in the said districts are
heavily fined; this is called a *khétia*.

But when all these sources of revenue have been
considered, the result is miserably out of proportion to
the expenditure, which includes immense civil and
military establishments, the erection of villages,
churches and schools, the making of roads and bridges
and other things absolutely necessary in a new colony.

It is the fashion of the radical and revolutionary

party in Algeria to cry out hotly against the expenditure for the military establishments in the country, and to attribute to them the want of cultivation of the land and all the other evils of which French colonists so bitterly complain. But I do not believe it possible to maintain the peace of the country without, for the Arabs, as a nation, have no respect for civilians. Count Ernest de Stackelberg, whose able memorandum I have already quoted with regard to the Kabyles, writes on this head :

'After a careful consideration of the subject, I have arrived at the conviction that without the constant presence of a strong military force it will be impossible for the French to hold Algeria. I should say that the present number (100,000 men) would be constantly required ; that, in fact, those figures should represent the *normal* state of the Algerian army, and that it could not be safely diminished for the following reasons :

'The French occupy forty-six towns or military stations without counting the villages, where garrisons would be required in case of the breaking out of hostilities. To diminish the number of these military outposts would be impossible, for in the Arab mind, to withdraw troops from any place would imply *fear* or *defeat.*'

Moreover, independently of the never-conquered spirit of the Kabyle tribes, the inhabitants of Morocco on the one frontier and of Tunis on the other, are perpetually fostering insurrections in Algeria, through the medium of those religious brotherhoods of which I have before spoken.

Again the Count writes :

'Although the Emperor of Morocco may be personally friendly to French interests, his people are not so. They are desperate fanatics, hating all Christians and especially the French.

' The empire itself is in a state bordering on anarchy, and the sovereign's authority is scarcely acknowledged except in the towns and on the sea-coast. To the south of Fez, the Morocco Berbers are completely independent, and the treaty concluded by the Emperor with the French has lowered him greatly in the esteem and consideration of his subjects.'

The question then arises : if such large military establishments be required, involving so large an annual deficiency in the budget, is the colony worth preserving ? The answer must be found in its mineral riches and in the uncontestable fertility of the soil. But that brings us again to the question of colonisation. On this head Count de Stackelberg writes :

' There is an axiom of which no one will dispute the truth, that to found a colony one must have colonists. Yet these are what are really wanting in Algeria.

' To cultivate this wonderfully rich soil, and to transform it into a paradise of agricultural wealth, few have yet been sent but public-house keepers, purveyors of

" restaurants," ruined manufacturers or swindlers! The government has given itself inconceivable pains to create villages and to establish families in them, but on the other hand it has committed some flagrant blunders. It expected to gather the fruits where the seeds were scarcely yet sown! It taxed every article of consumption instead of giving every possible immunity from taxation. It established so severe a Custom-house at the different ports that French commerce was positively paralysed. It wearied the new citizens with the duties of a National Guard, which were useless in a country full of regular troops. . . . In fact, until now, the enormous sums expended to establish this new colony may be said to have been well nigh wasted. The army made roads and built villages, and the houses are pretty and bright enough, but that is all. These colonists, although imported at so high a rate, found agriculture hard, distasteful, up-hill work, requiring a year or two's patient labour to produce any sort of return—so they gave it up. They became coffee-house and cook-shop keepers, or dealers in wine and spirituous liquors, and sub-let their grants of land to the very Arabs who had been driven out for their sakes. It seems difficult to believe, but I was told that the only crop which those colonists ever produced was the hay which they sold to the cavalry purveyors and which gave them no trouble except to mow.'

This severe picture is almost as true now as the day it was written. The only amelioration is in the diminution of the port dues and taxes. But to establish a colony on a sound footing three things are required—*security, capital,* and *hands.* And all three are more or less wanting in Algeria.

To do the French justice, we must allow them the palm for two things, making roads, and building towns. Some of the former are wonderfully well engineered, and of the latter nothing can be brighter, cleaner, or better laid out. But the stability of the houses is more doubtful and some are already crumbling into ruins. That, however, may be attributed to the mania for speculation in that particular branch of industry at one time, owing to the high price of lodgings. I was told of one man who built a house with money borrowed at thirty per cent. saying that the letting of it for one year would repay him both interest and capital. Of course, the supply of such houses soon exceeded the demand. When the Prussian war came the price of lodgings fell to next to nothing, and one bankruptcy after another followed in rapid succession.

Of the European population, upwards of 100,000 are Italians, Spaniards, Maltese and Mahonais, the latter being the most useful fraction of the whole. They are really an industrious people, and occupy themselves chiefly in market gardening; they are also

excellent coachmen. There are very few German families; whether the climate affects them or not I do not
know, but they are far less successful in Algeria than
in America, or Australia, or any other colony. But the
real misfortune of Algeria is that she has been invaded
by a swarm of adventurers, speculators, broken-down
tradesmen, or political refugees—men with neither
capital nor character, and utterly unscrupulous as to
ways and means. Perhaps a new era may dawn upon
her from the expatriation of so many good and honest
men from Alsace and Lorraine, and that thus out of a
great political crime may eventually be evolved a vast
moral improvement in this beautiful colony.

To sum up what I have said. Algeria contains within
herself the elements of one of the finest countries in the
world, for she has two hundred leagues of sea-board,
fine harbours, a magnificent soil, a beautiful climate,
and untold mineral riches; but from want of sufficient
security, capital and labour, these advantages have as
yet been little utilised.

France cannot establish a military colony, for it would
be contrary to the nature of her government or the
character of her people. Nor has she, as yet, been
able to establish a civil colony, because she cannot
transplant all at once, a patient, laborious agricultural
race, such as is needed in that vast field of untilled

ground. The real agriculturist, the true French peasant, possessing his snug homestead and his little capital, would never dream of permanently exchanging the Department where he was born and where he is happy and satisfied, for the burning suns of Africa, where he would be continually worried by the Arabs, if even the prospect of increased profits induced him to try the venture for a short time. I never spoke to a Frenchman in the colony that he did not allude to the time when he should have made sufficient money to return to 'la belle France.' Unlike our own people, they never look upon the colony as *home*, and therefore care less for its ultimate prosperity. But let us hope that a change will arise from the very misfortunes of France, and that another ten or twenty years may see a great alteration for the better in the colonisation and cultivation of this beautiful land, once the granary of Rome and of Europe. After all, every colony has difficulties to contend with in the beginning, and it often takes a generation of doubtful characters before you engender one of honest men.

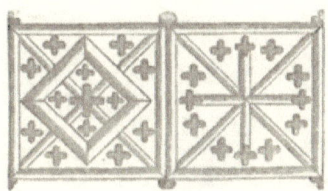

STONE WINDOW IN MOSQUE AT SIDI OKBAR.

R

CHAPTER IX.

TUNIS AND CARTHAGE.

T was the morning of Holy Thursday when, after an early service in St. Augustine's Cathedral, we were hurried on board the Messageries Impériales steamer 'Sinaï,' and steamed off in a few minutes for Tunis. Even things we do not like are melancholy if done for 'the last time,' and we were really sad at wishing good-bye to the French colony where we had spent such a happy winter and spring, and whose inhabitants had treated us everywhere with such genuine kindness and hospitality. Our fellow-passengers were of many lands—one, (a large Irish family,) seeking for health for an eldest son; another, a clever and amusing French doctor, who had been all over the world, and told anecdotes of an endless variety of countries; a third, an Arab, with a pretty little girl, proceeding to join his family at Tripoli. There are few things more amusing than the large and motley company into which one is thrown on occasions

like these, provided the sea be not too rough to enjoy
it. The evening passed quietly and calmly enough as
we coasted past Cape Rosa and so on to La Calle,
famous for centuries for its lakes, its cork woods, and
its coral fisheries. We did not see these fisheries in
operation, but the following description of them was
given us by the captain. A piece of wood is made in
the shape of a cross about a foot long, to the centre of
which a heavy stone is attached, which makes it fall to
the bottom of the sea; little nets of strong hemp are
attached to each arm of the cross, which is held hori-
zontally by means of a string lowered into the sea, and
the other end of which is fastened to the boat. When
the boatmen feel that the cross has touched the bottom,
they row backwards and forwards over the coral beds,
while the stone detaches the coral from the rocks,
which falls into the little nets, or remains hanging to
the arms of the cross. Upwards of two hundred boats
are thus engaged at one time, half of which are
Spanish; and the value of the coral thus brought up
in one year amounted to 152,800 francs.

Soon after we had passed the rock 'Rous' (or red
rock), just beyond La Calle, it became dark and began to
blow a gale, which continued to increase as we rounded
Cape Farina and so steamed into the harbour of
Goletta. We cast anchor at three in the morning and
got up eagerly, hoping to land before the swell

increased ; but it rained in torrents and the Consul's
servants in consequence did not hurry themselves to
bring the boat alongside, so that it was six o'clock
before we clambered with great difficulty from the rock-
ing deck of the ' Sinaï ' into the barge which the dragoman had at last brought to convey us ashore. Landing
at Goletta, it was again half an hour before the carriage
was ready, and by this time we were nearly soaked to
the skin.   However, there was no help for it, but to
start on the weary ten miles drive which still divided
us from the Consul's comfortable and hospitable house;
though, when we at last reached Tunis, we were as
miserable a set of women as could well be conceived.[1]
The kindness of the whole family, and a good fire
to dry our dripping clothes, soon made us forget our
troubles, and we then hurried up the little narrow street
to the Capuchin church, as it was Good Friday.   The
church was crammed to suffocation with Maltese women
in their black ' habbarahs,' as at Cairo, while the ' tre
ore d'agonie ' was being preached ; and a moving repre-
sentation of the dead Christ lay in a side chapel, the feet
of which were reverently kissed by the congregation
both before and after the ' tenebre.'

   Nothing can be more spacious and comfortable than
the consular residence, in which, through Mr. Wood's

---

[1] Since this was written, a railroad has been made from Goletta to
Tunis, and so on to the Bardo and to Marsa.

great kindness, we found ourselves installed. It looks
upon a little 'place,' near the Goletta Gate, with a
picturesque minaret, and a narrow street leading to the
'sooks' (or bazaars) on one side, and on the other,
the busy market-place, with the beautiful Bay of
Tunis, and the fine-shaped mountains beyond. There
is a long covered balcony glazed in, leading from one
of the drawing-rooms, which was a never-ending place
of interest and amusement to us, from the endless
variety of picturesque figures continually passing in
the 'place' below.

The following morning we paid our visit to the
'sooks,' those wonderful bazaars which rival, if they do
not surpass those of Cairo, Damascus and Constantinople. There is a glorious mosque and court in their
very midst, the domes of which are a marked feature
in all distant views of the town. But no profane foot
is ever allowed to cross the threshold or even to ascend
the three or four steps leading to the outer gateway.
We were told a story of a poor Jew whose 'shasheeah'
(or red cap) had been taken off and mischievously
thrown by a boy into the court, and who, without thinking, had rushed in to rescue it; but before he could
reach the spot where it had fallen he was murdered by
the indignant Mussulmen, who had all poured out of
their stalls in an instant, armed with sticks and stones,
to avenge the pretended sacrilege. The fanaticism of

this country, in fact, far exceeds that of any we
had yet visited, and in the interior, even the most
powerful protection scarcely avails to save a Christian
traveller from insult.   But to return to the sooks.
Ranged in little stalls above and below these covered
ways, with their coloured pillars and deep archways,
are squatted a multitude of men weaving or embroidering the most beautiful stuffs, scarfs of the most exquisite
shades, leather of every description, haïks, burnouses,
silks, and cloths of the softest and tenderest colours—
sea-green, pimento, pale rose, soft primrose, in fact,
every shade which would delight the heart of a painter,
but which are not to be found or matched in any city
of Europe.   Our first purchase, however, was not silk,
but a specimen of one of the most famous Tunis
manufactures, i.e., the 'shasheeahs,' or red caps, universally worn by every class, and dyed with a mixture
of cochineal and alum in the fountain of Zouwan, about
forty miles from Tunis, which particular spring is
supposed to give permanency to the colour.   They
are then lined and blocked in the 'sooks,' made up
according to the size required and ornamented with
the universal blue tassel, which is made of Constantino-
politan silk and sold by the weight.   The cheapest
'shasheeahs' cost thirty shillings, but some are much
dearer; they last, however, for ever.   Opposite this
stall was that of a dealer in incense and essences.   I

bought a tiny bottle of jessamine, which only contained
a few drops and was sealed up to prevent evaporation,
in spite of which, its subtle perfume escaped in a few
weeks. Then I tried the different kinds of incense and
finally chose some delicious stuff called Iowy Meccawy,
as it comes from Mecca, and looks like a brown rock
with white spar in it. It costs four piastres a pound,
or 2s. Then, passing through another bazaar filled with
silks and stuffs of different kinds, where we could not
resist making many little purchases, we came to the
leather department, where every description of shoe,
slipper, trappings for horses and mules, harness for
carriages, powder pouches, bags, &c., were most exquisitely embroidered, both in gold and in different
coloured silks ; some of the harness being quite wonderful, both in design and execution. This bazaar led to a
beautiful fountain just outside the town, from whence
there is a lovely view. The water is brought from the
Zaoughan mountain, which is such a feature in every
Tunisian landscape ; but the sun was so hot that
we were glad to return again to the shade of the
' sooks.'

After leaving the leather bazaar, we visited the
jewellers' courts, which, as at Cairo, are darker and
narrower than any others. Unfortunately, being the
Feast of the Passover, all the best shops were shut, as
they are kept almost entirely by the Jews. ' Toby,'

however, the well known dragoman of the Consulate, promised to bring us some specimens of their work ; a promise faithfully fulfilled.

In the afternoon, Mrs. Wood drove us into the country, passing under a beautiful old aqueduct, and by the Bardo or Bey's Palace, to pay a visit to some Moorish friends of hers, the Princess ———. The mother was a grand old lady with straight features, and a handsome though melancholy face. Two of her daughters-in-law were seated on a divan near her, and three lovely little grand-children. All were dressed in the universal costume of the Moorish ladies, which consists of a soft gauze chemise, a very short silk jacket, called a 'jubba,' of exquisite colour, either bright green, pink, yellow, or lilac; tight-fitting drawers, and a raised edifice or horn at the back of the head, into which the hair is gathered, and round which is wound a bright silk handkerchief, generally striped with gold ; while a kind of gauze scarf or lappet falls on the neck and shoulders. This dress is beautiful for children, but very peculiar for grown-up women, the 'jubba' not reaching much below the waist, so that the effect was not pleasing. Going afterwards to the male quarters of the house, we saw the husband of the princess—a magnificent old man, with long white hair, and with a head which Titian or Rembrandt would have delighted in painting. His poor little grandson was also there, a nice boy of eight ; but of their sad family history I must not speak.

After taking leave of them, we went on to another country house, which had an entrance-hall beautifully worked in that peculiar kind of stucco called by the Moors 'mukseh-hadeedah.' A thick coat of plaster is laid on the wall, and when set, the workman traces different intricate patterns on the surface, and cuts out the parts required with a sharp knife. It hardens quickly like stone, and looks like the most beautiful lace-work of white marble. Mrs. Wood told me that this kind of work is rapidly done, and certainly the effect is quite marvellous.

This house belonged to an amiable young princess, lately dead, and we were allowed to see the rest of the apartments, in which the doors, cupboards, and ceilings were beautifully carved. But the whole looked like a lovely cage, as it really was. The women here are hardly ever allowed to go out, not even to the mosques, and very rarely to see their relations ; when they do, it must be in a close carriage with all the blinds drawn down. Even among the peasant class, in passing the villages, not a single woman was visible. Their houses are all arranged in the Moorish fashion, with open courts, beautiful marble columns, arcades and galleries, the lower half of the walls being covered with tiles, of that brightly-coloured, highly-glazed kind

which I have so often described, and which seems
universal wherever the Moors have set their foot.
Adjoining this palace was one of the large rose
gardens for which the country is famous, and which
are a profitable investment in Tunis from the quantity
of 'attar' manufactured there.　On the road we
passed strings upon strings of camels, which here are
the universal beasts of burden, and are better treated
than the wretched mules and donkeys, from being so
much more valuable.　They have a curious fashion
for their carriage horses, if white, of staining three of
their legs and also their tails, bright orange colour,
with a preparation of henna, which had a most peculiar
effect.　I asked why they did not stain all four alike,
but was told that would be very unlucky!

This being Holy Saturday, quantities of cannon
were fired off when the bells were rung at the 'Gloria
in Excelsis,' and some so near the church that it
seemed as if they were about to bombard it.　The
devotion of the Catholics here is very striking, but
very demonstrative, as with most Southern nations.

After church on Easter-day, I went to see the
Superior of the Capuchins, a venerable old man, and a
native of France, who was very kind and introduced
me to the bishop.　He showed me a MS. account
which he had written, of the whole history of the
mission since St. Francis founded it in 1219.　They

have been in Tunis ever since, and have opened
churches and schools in all the towns of the Regency.
Mussulman fanaticism alone hinders a large increase
in the number of conversions to Christianity. Not
long ago a young Moor, who had become a natura-
lised Piedmontese subject, was secretly baptized with
his bride, and arrangements were in progress for their
leaving Tunis and settling in Malta, when they were
suddenly betrayed, dragged before the Bey, and put
to death before the Sardinian Consul had time to
interfere on their behalf. The young man was
strangled, and the poor girl sewn up in a sack and
thrown into the lake. No wonder that extra faith and
courage are required for men to profess Christianity in
this country.

The Sisters of St. Joseph 'of the Apparition' (my
old Jerusalem friends) have a large orphanage here,
together with a hospital and day schools. They have
nineteen sisters at work, but their convent is small
and must be very hot in summer.

In the afternoon Mrs. Wood again kindly drove us
out into the country, to introduce us to one of the
first Mussulman families in Tunis, who have a palace
about four miles from the town. Their name is Sidi
Hammeda Ben Ayat.[1]

[1] For the information of those who have not been in the East, I
should explain that 'sidi' is equivalent to our 'lord' and 'lilli'
to 'lady.'

They have a beautiful large Moorish house and
garden, with the usual courts and pillars and spacious
staircases.   But it was almost impossible to believe
that you were looking at a scene of every-day life
when you were ushered in to a room full of ladies,
children and slaves, all dressed in the most gorgeous
and beautiful colours and jewels, but in the peculiar
costume I have before mentioned.   They all had the
pointed black cap ('cufia'), and hanging down behind it
seven beautifully-embroidered tails called 'hiaout';
while round their heads they wore a bright scarf ('shorbat'), and over that again a gauze handkerchief ('beshkir').   The rest of their dress consisted of a soft gauzy
kind of chemise ; a delicious-coloured 'jubba' or vest,
made of catlan, a peculiar kind of silk of the softest
make, and most exquisite shades of colour : one green,
one pink, one yellow, one lilac, &c., with drawers of
gold or silver tissue fitting tight to the shape ; stock-
ings of the same material, and embroidered shoes.
One of the ladies good-naturedly put on a dress to
show us, in which the 'jubba,' trousers, 'shorbat' and
'beshkir' were all of exquisite silver stuff, heavy with
embroidery ; but it must be terribly cumbersome and
hot to wear.   When they went into the garden they
threw over their dresses what they called a 'suf-sary,'
which is a species of exquisitely fine white gandoura or
haïk.   The children had gold chains of a peculiar kind

round their heads, formed by interlacing circles of
metal, with Mahomet's hand and Solomon's seal
fastened on one side and hanging over the ear.   Even
the negresses had costly bracelets, and wore a species
of red and yellow striped silk jacket, the brilliant colouring of which set off their dark skins wonderfully.
The little children were beautiful, and so were two
of the daughters of the house; only rather too fat for
European taste.   They had dark almond-shaped eyes,
beautiful arched eye-brows, dark hair, and brilliant
complexions.   But I am bound to say that their
costume, especially when a number of them are seen
together, is the reverse of graceful or becoming, and
rather jars on our sense of modesty.

It would not, in fact, be possible for ladies to appear
so in public; but then, one must always remember
that they never quit their harems, and that such
things as petticoats or skirts are unknown to them.
It was a great disappointment to us to be unable to
talk to any of our amiable entertainers, as they knew
no tongue but Arabic.   Our deficiencies were, however, supplied by our kind hostess, Mrs. Wood, and
the Vice-Consul's wife, Mrs. Green, both of whom
acted as our interpreters, their long residence in that
country enabling them to speak its language with the
greatest ease and fluency.

The following morning we started on a charming

expedition across country, to see a coursing match. Arabs led the dogs in leash, which were of a kind very like our Scotch deer-hounds. Hawks are likewise used in this sport, and they hunt both hares and jackals. Our trysting-place was an old palace of the Beys called 'M'hammed-dieh,' a gorgeous pile of buildings, erected only a few years ago, but now entirely abandoned and left to rack and ruin. They have a superstition against living in a palace where one of their predecessors has died. Hence each Bey builds himself a fresh house, furnishes it, regardless of expense; and then, should he unfortunately happen to die there, the place is at once given up and deserted, and with it all the out-buildings, which are so numerous in an oriental establishment and which at M'hammed-dieh, with the harem, form a perfect town, encircled by a high wall, but now grass-grown and desolate like all the rest. We were admitted with difficulty into the great entrance-hall, with its beautiful broken staircase and shattered furniture, telling so sad a tale of reckless expenditure and wanton neglect, and then pic-nicked under the ruins of the once gorgeous harem, where fragments of marble and coloured tiles were scattered about in every direction. Only a few half-starved Arabs and their children (who crowded round us, bringing live red-legged partridges for sale) were hutted in the great weedy courtyard, amidst the general devastation. Yet the position and view from hence were glorious, overlooking the salt lake and the grand lead mountains of Gibel Resas. Hard by was one of those picturesque water-wheels peculiar to the country called 'naouras,' and which are said to date from the times of the Romans. All over the vast plains we had traversed were remains of pillars, broken capitals, and tombs ; while an aqueduct, said to have been restored in Spanish times, stood out against the horizon like those with which our eyes are so familiar in the Campagna of Rome. Presently, Mr. Wood's two beautiful daughters came galloping up with the rest of the hunting party, having killed not a hare but a jackal, which, however, had taken terrible revenge on one of the deer-hounds, which was so torn and mauled that we had to carry him home in one of the carriages. The heat during this expedition was so great that M—— had to go to bed on her return, and was laid up for several days; which misfortune only served to enhance the care and kindness of our host and his family, who nursed her as if she were one of their own children.

A picnic to the Belvedere, a picturesque olive garden just outside the city walls, on a rising ground overlooking the whole town, was my only diversion the following day ; but it was quite amusement enough to look out of my window on the busy market-place below, just beyond which, picturesque groups of

camels were always squatted, and generally growling
in unison. The following evening we were asked to
a great dinner at those very Ben-Ayats whose beautiful
house and ladies we had been introduced to a few
days before. The repast was almost endless in length
and in variety of food, but there was no wine, that
being forbidden to women by Mahometan law. Afterwards we drove to the country house of the eldest
married daughter, which is fitted up with every
English and French luxury. Her garden was lovely,
and her husband, who spoke French fluently and had
been a good deal in Paris, gave us the most beautiful
nosegay of roses, geraniums, Cape jessamine, and
other delicious flowers.

A few days later, on a bright and beautiful
morning, we started from Tunis through the Goletta
gate, on our way to the ruins of Carthage. Long
files of camels stalked slowly alongside of us, and
rows of scarlet flamingos, with their long legs, stood
on the sand or fluttered on the sea-shore. After
about an hour's drive along the Goletta road, we
turned off to the left, and ascending a hill came
to the tomb and chapel of St. Louis (the ancient
Byrsa), which has lately been ceded to the French
Government. It is a large garden enclosed by a high
wall, and containing a quantity of columns, capitals,
torsos, and mosaics, which have been collected in the

neighbourhood ; while, on a raised terrace facing the sea, the chapel is built where St. Louis was interred. He is much venerated by the Moslems, who call him Sidi Bou Saed, and make regular pilgrimages to his tomb. The view from thence is perfectly lovely, overlooking the whole site and ruins of Carthage, with Goletta and the blue sea beyond. Here, on August 25, 1270, this saint-like monarch breathed his last, amidst the tears not only of his own family and people but of the whole of Europe. Here he gave those wonderfully wise instructions to his eldest son, a copy of which may still be seen in the Paris archives. His charity, humility, and perfect resignation, increased in his last moments, and with the words of the Psalmist on his lips : 'Lord, I will enter into Thine house, I will adore in Thy holy temple, and will give glory to Thy name,' his pure and holy soul exchanged this life for a better. The good woman who had the care of the sanctuary gave me some marble which had been found on this spot, and spoke with delight of the number of French people who yearly came to pray at his shrine. 'La pauvre France ! Il faut bien que le saint nous aide,' she added, for peace was not yet signed. From St. Louis's tomb we drove down to the ruins of Carthage. The first we visited were the cisterns, which were most curious and in wonderful preservation. They are an oblong mass of brickwork

forming a succession of covered arches and containing
eighteen reservoirs of water, each ninety-three feet in
length, and nineteen in breadth, with a depth of twenty-
seven feet six inches.   One or two of these reservoirs
have been excavated, and are full of water.   In some,
the steps still remain leading down to what I suppose
must have been baths, as there are fragments of little
chambers in the sides of the wall.   These reservoirs
are connected with some larger cisterns which we
visited afterwards, and also with the great aqueduct.
Part of the old Roman Mosaic pavement or road
remains, leading to the ruins of a large temple, through
which we walked, stumbling over broken columns
and fragments of marble, partly concealed in the long
grass, till we arrived at the port, of which huge portions of masonry and marble are still standing.   We
strolled for some time along the sea-shore, I, thinking
of St. Monica, for it was from hence that she strained
her eyes in vain after her boy's receding ship.   All
around us were gigantic blocks of stone lying in
different positions, and great plinths of marble, and
broken frieze and capitals, speaking of the glories of
the past.   Between this spot and Goletta were a
number of villas and country houses, or rather sea-side
watering-places of the Bey's family or his ministers;
and I can conceive no more enjoyable spot in the
summer-time than this sea-shore, with its big shady

rocks, beautiful sands, lovely shells, and glorious blue sea, to say nothing of the association with the past. Mrs. Wood told me that it was her children's greatest delight to come here for the day from their country house at Marsa which is only a few miles off, and I did not wonder at their taste. Remounting the hill we came to the ruins of the famous temple of Esculapius. The view from thence of the whole line of coast, with the range of mountains beyond, and the sparkling Mediterranean, was wonderfully beautiful. Then we passed by an old Moorish fort, and came to what was the old 'Magaria' or Faubourg of Carthage, close to which is the Arab village of Malakah, occupying the site of the great cisterns, which are now entirely choked up, but which were evidently connected with the eighteen smaller ones we had previously visited. These are 200 feet long, and also arched. They formed the termination of the great aqueduct, which brought spring-water to Carthage from the mountains of Zaghwan. Huge fragments of stone lie all along the plain, with broken arches, extending upwards of fifty miles. Here and there, these arches are perfect. A beautiful and very large Mosaic lion tearing a horse, was discovered not long ago, close to Mr. Wood's garden. In fact, it is impossible to dig anywhere without coming upon fragments of marble and Mosaic; but the government are very jealous of any such excavations, and a poor man who had brought a fine piece of Mosaic to light the other day was severely bastinadoed.

After rambling about among the ruins as long as the heat would permit, we drove on to Marsa, the country palace of the English consul, which is a large and handsome building, with fine palms and cypresses, and an arched colonnade, done in that beautiful 'mukseh-hadeedah' or stucco work, which I admire so much. There is a beautiful large garden adjoining the house, and at the end a picturesque 'naoura,' which was worked by a camel. From the tower above there is a glorious view over the whole country. There we had our luncheon and rested during the heat of the day; after which we went to pay a visit to the niece of the Bey, who was on the eve of her marriage, and whose mother had kindly invited us to see the preparations for her wedding. We drove about a mile beyond the Marsa, to a large palace with an outer court, where every arrangement was being made for a 'fantasia' or exhibition of horsemanship, which was to form part of the bridal festivities. We were received by the princess in an alcoved room with a marble floor and divans all round, opening out of the 'patio' as usual; and after coffee and sweetmeats, were taken to an inner apartment, where the bride's presents and trousseau were laid out for inspection. The magnificence of everything far exceeded my expectations. No European trousseau could be compared with it for gorgeousness of material, infinite variety, beauty of colour, or finish of embroidery. Then they showed us the upper rooms where the marriage feast was prepared, consisting of every possible variety of cake, biscuit, pistachio nuts, almonds, sugar-plums, preserved fruits and confectionery, and that in such quantities that it seemed as if no amount of wedding guests could possibly consume a tenth of it. Then we returned to the patio, where a concert had been prepared for us of the usual Arab instruments, performed by twenty or thirty of the prettiest slaves in the establishment, all beautifully dressed. And then followed a dance, part of which consisted in wriggling the body in such a way that it appeared as if the stomach of the dancer was independent of the rest of her person, and to our intense astonishment it ended in a succession of somersaults, or turning head over heels several times in succession, after the manner of the small boys in the streets. We did not see the bride, as it was the etiquette for her to remain shut up for seven days before her marriage, during which time she was invisible even to her father.

Great preparations were going on for putting on the henna that evening, which is a vegetable powder made into a paste, with which, on the eve of all important festivals, they paint their toe and finger nails a bright orange colour. I was very sorry that we were unable to stay for the conclusion of the wedding ceremonies, which must have been like a scene in the 'Arabian Nights.' But when all is said and done, the position of women in this country is deplorable. To bathe and dress, to smoke and eat, are their sole occupations. Hardly any can read or write, and their time hangs so heavily on their hands that the greatest kindness you can do is to go and pay them a visit, if only to kill half an hour or so. Of religion they seem to know absolutely nothing. But, of course, it was difficult to ascertain their real feelings on any subject, when every word was obliged to be delivered through an interpreter. Their beauty is undeniable, and the mother of the little princess had a delicate high-bred face and a gentle courtesy of manner which would have done honour to any European court. Her sister-in-law, the wife of one of the other Beys who was there, was also very handsome and covered with beautiful jewels.

We did not see the palace of the reigning Bey at Goletta; but were told that it was not remarkable for beauty or splendour of decoration. The Bardo, however, which is his palace near Tunis, is a very fine pile of building with a beautiful marble staircase guarded by eight marble lions : columns arcaded with black and white marble, and cloisters and ceilings of that beautiful mukseh-hadeedah work which I have so often mentioned as peculiar to the country. In the throne-room were full-length oil portraits of all the crowned heads in Europe, except of our own Queen Victoria, who, unfortunately, in return for the gorgeous presents sent her by the Bey, only forwarded a little ordinary print of herself, to the great mortification of the English Consul, and I may add of all English people visiting the Regency. One cannot help hoping that this mistake may some day be rectified and that our own beloved Sovereign may take her place with the rest of the European potentates.

Our happy visit at Tunis was now drawing to a close. One thing only had marred our enjoyment, and that was the mosquitoes! No amount of precaution, no careful evening visit to the closely fastened down net, no burning of insect powder by the faithful black 'Fatma,' availed to drive away our ubiquitous perse-cutors, who made our nights a burden to us, no less by their painful stings than by their hopelessly worrying hum, whenever we tried to forget their presence in sleep. The only compensation was in the early rising which our tormentors made inevitable—for nothing could be more delicious than to open one's window and see the glorious African sunrise gilding the mountain-tops, and throwing gorgeous lights on the lake, and the forts on its banks. Mountain and lake,

which five minutes before had been of the richest purple
hue, melted as the sun rose into the purest gold
colour.   Then used to begin the din in the camel
market under my window—a din so overpowering that
in any other country an *émeute* would have been appre-
hended, and the advent of at least half-a-dozen special
constables.   Hundreds of Moors stood and haggled
together, all screaming and gesticulating at the tops of
their voices, the braying of the mules and the growling
of the camels adding to the concert, together with the
cackling of the wretched fowls, who, heads downwards, were strung over donkeys' necks, regardless of
their sufferings.   By degrees the bustle and noise of
the market were lulled, the camels were driven home
again, and then a multitude of black figures would be
seen wending their way to the early services in the old
cathedral.   That last day, we took one more walk in
the 'sooks' with our faithful guide, the consular dragoman, 'Toby' (now alas! no more), to whose intelligence
and honesty we were indebted for most of the silken
treasures we bore away with us from this land of
beautiful colours.   This time our purchases consisted of
some of the beautiful-shaped pottery of the place, including a wonderful high green lamp to stand on the
ground, a 'tum-tum,' and a small incense burner,
likewise of green pottery, and though very coarse and
cheap, of a most picturesque shape.

We also drove to the public promenade, where towards evening, all the rank and fashion of Tunis are
assembled ; and ended by visiting Toby's wife and
sisters, who were most gorgeously dressed in Moorish
fashion, and who presented us with some delicious
dates for our journey. And then, sorrowfully taking
leave of those who had been so kind to us, we drove
down to Goletta, and at half past five rowed for the
last time under the windows of the harem and past the
Bey's ugly palace, till we reached the steamer ' Milano '
which had already raised her anchor and was ready to
start. At six o'clock we sorrowfully watched the
receding African shore after four months of great enjoyment among its varied races, and coasting by Marsala
and Trapani, reached Palermo after a calm and unevent-
ful passage of forty-five hours.

BISKRA EAR-RING

T

LONDON : PRINTED BY
SPOTTISWOODE AND CO., NEW-STREET SQUARE
AND PARLIAMENT STREET

www.ingramcontent.com/pod-product-compliance
Lightning Source LLC
Chambersburg PA
CBHW021039030726
47496CB00006B/1618